Peter Ackroyd

The FALL of TROY

Peter Ackroyd is a master of the historical novel:
The Last Testament of Oscar Wilde won the Somerset
Maugham Award; *Hawksmoor* was awarded both
the Whitbread Novel of the Year and the *Guardian*
Fiction Prize; and *Chatterton* was shortlisted for the
Booker Prize. His most recent historical novel was
The Lambs of London. He is also the author of
Shakespeare: The Biography and the Ackroyd's Brief
Lives series.

ALSO BY PETER ACKROYD

FICTION

The Great Fire of London

The Last Testament of Oscar Wilde

Hawksmoor

Chatterton

First Light

English Music

The House of Doctor Dee

Dan Leno and the Limehouse Golem

Milton in America

The Plato Papers

The Clerkenwell Tales

The Lambs of London

NONFICTION

*Dressing Up: Transvestism and Drag:
The History of an Obsession*

London: The Biography

Albion: The Origins of the English Imagination

Shakespeare: The Biography

The
FALL
of
TROY

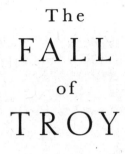

The
FALL
of
TROY

A NOVEL

PETER

ACKROYD

Anchor Books
A Division of Random House, Inc.
New York

FIRST ANCHOR BOOKS EDITION, NOVEMBER 2008

The Library of Congress has cataloged the Nan A. Talese edition as follows:
Ackroyd, Peter.
The fall of Troy : a novel / Peter Ackroyd.—1st ed.
p. cm.
1. Archaeologists—Fiction. 2. Women archaeologists—Fiction.
3. Troy (Extinct city)—Fiction. I. Title.
PR6051.C64F35 2007
823'.914—dc22 2007007208

Book design by Amanda Dewey

Anchor ISBN: 978-0-307-38649-6

www.anchorbooks.com

Printed in the United States of America
10 9 8 7 6 5 4 3 2 1

The

FALL

of

TROY

ONE

He fell down heavily on his knees, took her hand and brought it up to his mouth. "I kiss the hand of the future Mrs. Obermann." He spoke in English. Neither she nor her parents understood German, and he disliked speaking demotic Greek. He considered it vulgar.

Sophia Chrysanthis looked down at his bald head, and noticed a small scar. "You have been wounded, Heinrich."

"A fragment of the statue of Zeus. On the island of Ithaca. That is where I found the palace of Odysseus, the wanderer. I discovered the chamber where his wife, Penelope, had woven her endless tapestry. She was always faithful to him. You will be my Penelope, Sophia."

"I hope you do not travel as far as Odysseus."

"You will never leave my side." He rose, with difficulty, and bowed to her parents, who were standing together by the window. "I will utter prayers for you every day. If I live to be a thousand years old, I will never forget you." Outside, in the dusty light, the horses and carriages passed along the avenues; he glimpsed three women, holding up parasols to protect themselves from the bright sun of the early Athenian spring, chattering together as they walked upon the cobbles. They were dressed in pale green, with white veils and bonnets, and he knew at once that they were sisters. "This is an auspicious day. Your daughter will be a partner in my labours. She will be cherished by Greece."

"She has no greater desire than to be your wife, Herr Obermann." Madame Chrysanthis gave a slight nod, as if making some formal remark for duty's sake. "We have taught her that a wife is but the shadow of her husband."

"The women in Germany would not believe you."

"That is why you are not marrying a German."

Obermann laughed. He already knew that Madame was a formidable woman, and he hoped that her daughter had inherited her sterner virtues. "But my wife will be my partner in uncovering the lost past of her country. She will stand within the walls of Troy!"

"Sophia has a passion for learning. That is true." Colonel Chrysanthis deemed it necessary to enter the conversation: the future of his only child was, after all, being discussed. "Ever since your first letter to us she has been reading Homer to me."

"She draws up maps of the battle lines," Madame Chrysanthis said.

"This is all good. All excellent." Obermann had once more taken Sophia by the hand. "She is another Athene, as learned as she is beautiful."

"I will not be a goddess, Heinrich."

"I cannot wait to bring you to the plain of Troy. To show you the place where Hector and Achilles fought. To show you the palace of Priam. And the walls where the Trojan women watched their warriors in battle with the invader, Agamemnon, and his soldiers. It will stir your blood, Sophia."

"It was a long time ago, Heinrich."

"Not for me. It is eternal. Beyond time."

"I do not know if I will be able to see so far."

"My wife will see everything."

———

A FEW DAYS EARLIER he had led her into the courtyard of the house, cool in the shadows of the evening, and sat with her on the marble

bench there. "I must have you, Sophia. Once I have come to a conclusion I cannot be moved. I am unshakeable. As soon as I saw your
photograph, I knew that I was yours."

"So you chose me without reason?"

"We do things because we do them. There is no necessary explanation. Your Greek dramatists knew this. Homer knew it."

"I thought that you wanted me because I am a woman who reads
Homer."

"That is a part of it. There we are already married. But there is
also fate, Sophia. As hard and as desperate as life."

———

THE CEREMONY was conducted in the little church of Hagios
Georgios, set back from the Odos Ermou in a small square, while the
servants of the Chrysanthis household prepared the wedding feast.
There was much discussion among them about the relative merits of
bride and groom. The maids considered him too old for Sophia. She
was in her mid-twenties, whereas Herr Obermann must be fifty, no,
more than fifty. He would soon be stout, and he wore pebble glasses;
he was short, too, with a great round head like a cannon ball.

"He speaks too loud," Maria Karmeniou said. "You can hear his
voice booming through the house."

"It is the German manner," Nikola Zannis explained. "They are
strong. Impatient."

The butler and the valet took his part. Miss Chrysanthis was
young—and some even called her beautiful—but she had a shocking
temper like her mother. She had been as sweet to him as the honey of
Hybla, but they prophesied that this would not last long after the wedding night. It was agreed by all of them, however, that Herr Obermann must have paid a very large dowry for his new wife. And, for
this, they were grateful. In recent months their employers had pared
down costs so much that they had had little opportunity of cheating
them.

The feast itself was lavish, of course, with all the sweet pastries and
dainty confections that are usual on such occasions. Obermann drank

a great deal of wine, and even called out for Bavarian beer; but there was none on the premises. Then before the meal was over, against all custom, he stood up and made a speech. He began by praising the beauty of Greek women, as exemplified by Madame Chrysanthis, who had presided over the most charming meal since Aphrodite dined with Zephyrus and the Nereides. Her consort, the great man Colonel Chrysanthis, the pride of the National Patriotic Army, who had fought so valiantly against the Asiatics, was especially worthy of praise; but he deserved most thanks for producing out of his powerful loins his most splendid daughter. "Will you raise your glasses to the young lady whom I have the honour to call Frau Obermann?" He picked up his own glass for the toast. "She will be my comrade in the field. Thanks to the exertions of her parents, she is a lover of learning. She has been an admirer of the Homeric poems since her earliest childhood, and has expressed to me her heartfelt sympathy with my task. When I return to the plain of Troy, as I shall do very shortly, I shall take with me a blessing greater than the Palladion that protected the old city!" At this point he began to recite from memory the passage of the *Iliad* in which the goddess, flashing-eyed Athene, instils courage and hope into the breast of mighty Diomedes. Only Sophia could understand a word of the ancient Greek. The others listened in perplexed silence as Obermann continued his oration.

When the meal was over, he danced wildly in the courtyard of the Chrysanthis house. Sophia stood with the other married women as he leaped into the air and threw out his arms, in imitation of the Turkish peasants whom he had seen in the small villages near Troy. He began to sweat dreadfully, and his bald head seemed to be melting in the rays of the afternoon sun. And Sophia thought, how can I love a man who dances so badly?

That night, after he and Sophia had retired to the marital chamber—the bed strewn with flowers, according to custom—the servant on that floor was awakened by the sound of howling. She hurried down the corridor and put her ear to the door of the Obermanns' chamber. The howling had stopped. But then she heard Herr Obermann singing, and there was a noise like that of feet banging on the wooden floor. She crossed herself, and went back to her room. She could not have known that this was a German marching song.

—⁓—

AT BREAKFAST the next morning, to her parents' evident surprise, Sophia greedily consumed all the bread and dates in front of her; she ate the cheeses and the potted tongue, and even nibbled at the olives, which she normally despised. She had in the past condemned them as "peasant food," but now she seemed to take a certain pleasure in biting into their taut black skin. Her husband ate very quickly, as was his habit, looking around at the others with wary eyes. He devoured his food as if it were about to be snatched from him. Now, for the first time, Sophia remonstrated with him. "You will do harm to your constitution, Heinrich. You eat too fast."

"There is nothing wrong with my constitution. I am tough. I am energetic. Who else do you know to swim in the sea at dawn? Or ride an hour before breakfast?" He rose early each morning and greeted the rising sun, stretching out his arms and welcoming "the rosy-fingered dawn," *rhododaktulos eos*; then he would ride down to the harbour at Cophos and plunge into the waters of the Saronic Gulf, to the amusement of the sailors and fishermen, who did not consider the sea to be a place of recreation. "And who are you to advise me about my health, Sophia? You drink too much coffee. It poisons the kidneys. Our children will be dwarves."

"Do you wish to see the *Gazette*?" the colonel asked him.

"No. It is barbaric Greek. Wait. Let me read the shipping news."

—⁓—

HE GREW LESS COURTEOUS to his parents-in-law in the days immediately after the wedding; with his wife, he also seemed less restrained. The struggle was over. He had gained, as always, the object he desired. It soon became clear, too, that he was impatient to leave. Every morning he looked in the shipping columns, to discover what ships had arrived and departed from Piraeus. He received telegrams every day from Constantinople and Kannakale; he read them eagerly, and tore them into little pieces. Then, at the end of their first week of marriage, he had visited the shipping agent and booked himself and his wife on the passage by steam-boat to the Dardanelles.

When he informed Sophia of this decision, she wept.

"Come now," he said, "this is your new life."

"I have never left Greece before, Heinrich. You must allow me a few tears."

"It is only natural in a woman. I grant you that. But Frau Obermann does not shed tears."

She looked at him for a moment, then wiped her eyes. "You will never see them again."

"Good. And now to business. We leave on Monday morning aboard the *Zeus*. I have taken an additional cabin for our luggage."

"And how long will we be gone?"

"Some months. The rains do not begin until December."

He had spoken to her already about his excavations at Hissarlik. He had left them in the charge of his Russian assistant; but, from the first days of his courtship of Sophia, he had been eager to return. "You ask me why it has become my obsession," he said to her one evening. "Why? Why is it considered to be the first city? Why is it the vision of the poets? Why has it haunted mankind for three thousand years? I do not know the answer to these things."

She realised soon enough that he did not enjoy being questioned, on that or any other subject; but, after a few glasses of wine, he would invariably furnish her with all the information she required. "Do you know the Cypriot proverb, Sophia," he had asked her a week before the wedding, " 'Son of a priest, grandson of the devil'?" He chuckled. "My father was a Lutheran pastor."

"I have heard the saying."

"It is true! But he was not an ordinary minister. He told me of trolls and fairies. Of ghosts and demons. Of treasure buried in the bowels of the earth."

"Is that what you are digging up?"

"No. I am digging for science, not for reward. And then, when I was about six years old, he began reading Homer to me. I did not understand the Greek, of course, but it was the music of the verse I loved. I became aware of the sound and the pattern. That is how I learned Arabic. And French, Greek, Russian, English, all of them came rolling off my tongue."

"You told me that your father had no education."

"And how did he become a minister? That is nonsense, my little Sophia. He educated himself in Greek." She was silent for a moment. "That is why I promised him to study Homer. It was not difficult for me. It is pure. It is the origin."

———∿∿———

HIS LETTER to the Chrysanthis family had been wholly unexpected. He had requested from a friend in Athens, Stephanos the surgeon, photographs of young women of his acquaintance who might make suitable brides. "Please see if you can find me a young woman," he wrote to Stephanos, "with a Greek name and a soul inspired by the history of her ancient land. I am a very good judge of faces, and my first impressions are never wrong." Among the photographs Stephanos supplied was one of Sophia, the daughter of his friend the colonel, and Obermann wrote back at once. "Sophia Chrysanthis is a splendid woman, easy to talk to, compassionate, kindly and a good housewife, full of life and well brought up. I see in her eyes a great inclination for learning, and I am certain that she will love and respect me." He also asked several questions. What property does Colonel Chrysanthis possess? How old is he and how many children does he have? How many male and how many female children? How old is Sophia? What is the colour of her hair? Does she play the piano? Does she speak foreign languages and, if so, which? Does she understand Homer and other ancient writers? The answers from Stephanos were entirely satisfactory: Sophia understood English and, more importantly, she read Homer with avidity. "I am overjoyed," he wrote to his friend. "I have wished for such a companion all my life. We will be married within three months." He immediately made plans to travel

to Athens for his first meeting with his intended bride. In his letter to
her parents, despatched from Constantinople, he enlarged upon her
obvious propensity for learning. He described his excavations at Troy,
and his previous excavations at Ithaca, "known to all the civilised
world." He also promised a dowry of fifteen thousand francs.

The colonel and his wife did not take long to agree to his propos-
als, but they took the precaution of consulting Sophia. "It is an unusual courtship," her mother told her, "but he means well."

"Am I to live abroad?"

"He refers to Paris and London. He has houses in both cities." She
did not mention the current excavations; Anatolia had a reputation
among the Greeks for lawlessness and barbarism. "He is an influen-
tial man, Sophia."

"Then I may learn to love him."

"You must try."

On his first arrival in Athens he brought with him a small perfume
bottle of terracotta, an owl-faced goblet and a gold figurine. "These
are tokens from Troy," he said to her in English, before greeting her
parents who stood behind her as if to prevent her retreat. "Salutations
from your ancestors!" He took them from the pockets of his overcoat.
"I carry things about my person. The Turks search my luggage when
I am asleep. So you are Sophia." He bowed low and kissed her hand.
"Do you see this little idol? The marks here signify her hair. It is the
goddess of fertility. It is yours. May we continue to speak English?"
Sophia was surprised by his volubility, and by his evident self-posses-
sion. "I am overjoyed to greet you. I give you this perfume bottle as a
symbol of purity. I give you this goblet as a symbol of fidelity. Guard
them well. They are priceless."

They drove back through the streets of Athens in a closed carriage,
but Obermann kept peering out the window at the city. "There are
the baths of Hera!" he said. "In no very good state of preservation.
There I see the ruins of the Periclean library. Where those beggars
are sitting." Sophia glanced at him from time to time. She was trying
to define him to herself, but at the moment she did not know his

limits. He jumped out of the carriage, after the other three had descended, and clapped his hands at the sight of the Chrysanthis mansion set back from the road in a garden of peach trees, almond trees and pear trees.

"It is a small house, Herr Obermann," Madame Chrysanthis said. "We are no longer important people."

"It is truly delightful, Madame. Enchanting. It is like the little palace of Eupeithes, mother of Antinous!"

That evening, after dinner had been taken away, Obermann sat in the drawing room and smoked a Turkish cigarette. He continued the conversation he had been conducting with Sophia's father. "Choose a commodity that is always needed, Colonel. Olive oil. Tea. Every night go down on your knees, like the Homeric warriors, and pray for a war. If you find a war, you will find a scarcity. When the American civil war began, I bought up all the cotton I could find."

"That war had an unfortunate outcome."

"Neither good nor bad, Colonel. Merely an opportunity. A different opportunity. Do you know my full name, dear Sophia?"

"I know I am to call you Heinrich."

"Johann Ludwig Heinrich Julius Obermann. Ludwig after Beethoven. Julius after Caesar. And do you know why Johann?" She shook her head. "After John the Baptist! I prophesy the future! That is why I was an excellent businessman." He got up and walked over to the window by the veranda. "And how do you contemplate life with such a man, my dear Sophia? I put the question to you in front of your parents, so there will be no misunderstandings."

"I do not believe that you are avaricious, Heinrich, if that is what you mean."

"No. That is not my humour, as the English say. What a pretty sky you have in Athens! But I am determined."

She suddenly felt a wave of exaltation. In the company of this man she would be carried forward. She would triumph with him. She turned to her mother, with the strangest smile upon her face. Madame Chrysanthis stared at her, then looked away.

"You have not answered my question, dear Sophia."

"Do you not see that I am smiling? That is my answer to you."

"A very charming answer." He walked over to her quickly, took her hand and kissed it. "If we continue like this, we will satisfy each other."

Two

The Obermanns left Piraeus on the overnight steamer; the captain of the *Zeus* had assigned his own valet to them for the short journey to the Dardanelles, but, by the time the young man had brought them coffee, just before dawn, Obermann was already pacing the deck and peering towards the east. "Where is my wife? She must see the dawn."

"I am already with you, Heinrich." Her voice came out of the shadows. "I also wish to see the dawn."

"You have never known the sea until now. There. Look there." The edge of the world was limned with light, and a red glow seemed to spread along the horizon. "The light is glorious. But when the circle of the sun appears, there is a wholly different sensation. There is a revelation." He shielded his eyes from the wind. "That is where our future lies, Sophia. We are sailing towards Troy."

"We are sailing away from home."

"Home is here. With me. I am your home. Look now. Have you ever seen such a colour before? The rising sun will sit upon a throne of blood." He turned to the valet. "Bring our breakfast on to the deck. We must feast on this. Such majesty."

Within a few minutes the boy brought out a plate of cold boiled hens' eggs. To Sophia's astonishment, Obermann took one and swallowed it whole. Then he took another. "When I was a child in Mecklenburg," he said, drinking down a cup of thick black coffee, "I dreamed of buried treasure. There was a small hill in our village. It was surrounded by a ditch and was no doubt a prehistoric burial place. You have no idea how many ancient tombs are still to be found in Europe, but nobody bothers with them. What we call *hünengrab*."

He rarely used German in her company, but, three days earlier, he had addressed a German couple in Syntagma Square; he seemed to her then to change his identity: he somehow became older, and smaller.

"But in our legends it was known that in this hill a robber-knight had buried his beloved child in a golden cradle. Oh, we were surrounded by treasures. There was a pond beside our schoolhouse, out of which a maiden was believed to rise each midnight, holding a silver bowl. Many times my father bitterly lamented his poverty. And I would say to him, 'Papa, why do you not dig up the golden cradle and the silver bowl? Then we will be rich.' He never replied. In our poverty he wished us to keep our fairy stories." To Sophia it seemed that his eyes were brimming with tears. But then he swallowed another egg. "I have always believed that my father poisoned my mother. Does that shock you? Yet I still loved him. I will tell you the story one day."

Sophia retreated to the cabin, on the excuse that she wished to find a handkerchief, and she sat down upon the narrow bed. She saw the Aegean stretching ahead, stirred now by a north-easterly wind, and knew that she had to begin her life again in the company of a stranger.

Obermann came back into the cabin. "My dearest Sophia, I have upset you. I have not been considerate. Forgive me."

"What is there to forgive, Heinrich?"

"We should not dwell upon the past." He burst out laughing. "But who am I to say this? I am an archaeologist!" Then he took her up in his arms and, in the tiny space, danced a waltz with her to imagined music. And she thought, as she danced, "Well, at least I shall not be bored with you."

By the middle of the morning they had passed the island of Khios, and Sophia glimpsed the coast of Turkey lying eastwards. She could see small settlements—fishing villages, no doubt—and she could hear the barking of dogs. She did not mind the motion of the sea; if anything, it comforted her. This ceaseless rocking was like a cradling. "Do you see there, Sophia, that bay? That is where the princess Hesione was exposed to the attacks of the sea-monster sent by Neptune. Do you see the promontory of black rock? That is where Hercules saved her. There is the trench he built." There was a ridge leading inland from the promontory.

"You believe these stories, Heinrich."

"There is truth to them. We live in a hard age. An age of iron. We need these stories. We should give thanks that they survive." He went over to the rail and watched the seagulls as they flew beside the boat. "This is the path that Helle and Phryxus took when they flew on the ram with the golden fleece. How I loved that story! They crossed the Aegean Sea, as we do, north-eastwards. You did not know the region was so blessed? How could you know such things? Half the stories of the world begin here. That is why I came. See how the birds dip their wings in the current of the wind. Helle grew frightened by the waves beneath her, and fell away from the golden fleece. The water where she drowned became known as the Hellespont."

"There is no need to worry, Heinrich. I will never fall."

"You have no fear of great heights?"

"I have no fear of falling. That was the cause of her distress."

"You rewrite the myths of your own country! You are a splendid creature!"

An English clergyman, with a black ebony cane, was standing close to the rail of the deck; he had been listening eagerly to their conversation. "Do I have the great good fortune of addressing Herr Obermann?"

"You do."

"I attended your lecture at Burlington House last year. It was a revelation, sir."

He was very tall, and seemed to lean forward as he spoke. He had a low resonant voice, and a curious weakness in his eyes that made him blink continually. "I was a Grecian at university, Herr Obermann, but in that hour I learned more of Greece than in the whole of my previous life."

"Oh! Do you hear that, Sophia? This reverend sir is my disciple!"

"Harding, sir. Decimus Harding."

Obermann had given three lectures at the Society of Antiquaries in Burlington House on the origins of the Greek race, which he traced to the ancient settlers of northern Europe. He told how the tribes of hunter-gatherers had moved down upon the virgin soil of Asia Minor and Anatolia, where they learned the arts of farming. There emerged villages based upon the ties of kinship, where simple pottery was manufactured and where mats or baskets were woven. Some of these villages began to gather together and, over a thousand years, they grew naturally into small towns. He had a vision of the world where all people were embarked upon a long journey. All phases of world history were in equilibrium. In these towns distinctions of wealth and strength became evident; there arose leaders and ruling families who built large houses or fortified dwellings. Over many generations the towns became cities.

For Obermann the city was the high point of the world, the destination to which all people travelled. The Greek city-state, the *polis,* was thus the product of thousands of years of striving and competition. "I think of a street in sixth-century Athens or Corinth," he had told the Society of Antiquaries, "as a street in London or Paris or New York! It is the same civilisation. Yet forgive me. I speak as if a thousand years might pass in a moment, but archaeology tells us a different story. A moment of fear when a hoard of jewellery is hidden beneath a stone, a moment of peril when fire blackens the walls of a house, a moment of death when an arrowhead pierces a skull—these are the moments that an archaeologist uncovers. For the people who lived and suffered there were no thousands of years, only the brief span of a human lifetime in which little of any consequence may have occurred." There was an interruption of coughing in several parts of the room. "The shards of broken pottery that I find scattered all over the earth are signs of ordinary human existence that hardly seems to alter. And yet how vast are the changes seen by the ancient historian! That is the task of the archaeologist—to bring together the infinitely great and the infinitely small. How can a moment's thoughtfulness or anxiety, fading upon a face almost as soon as it has arisen, be connected with the creation of a pyramid or a great wall? There is the paradox, gentlemen."

It had become clear to Decimus Harding, among others in the audience, that Obermann had left to one side the question of religion. But then he began to talk of shamans and witch-doctors, in which direction the clergyman was happy to follow him. Harding imagined himself, for a moment, dancing around his parishioners in Broad Street, Oxford, dressed only in a loin-cloth.

"I am delighted to make your acquaintance, Reverend Harding. The English love my work. They treat me like a lord!" He rolled out the last phrase, in imitation of an English accent. "You know that Mr. Gladstone came to hear me on the subject of Homer? It was a great moment in my life."

"Mr. Gladstone is a scholar."

"Of course he is. He perfectly accepts my theories. He understands that I am about to solve the greatest mystery in the world. 'If I could accompany you to Troy,' he said to me, 'I would give five years of my life.' This is from your prime minister!"

"I do not doubt it."

Harding had a large mole upon his left cheek. Sophia tried to ignore it, but could not resist hasty little glances.

"Do not doubt. There, Sophia, do you see the small island ahead of us? That is where Achilles came to meet Polyxena." He turned back to Decimus Harding, and put his hand upon the clergyman's shoulder. "The English revere me. In France they believe Troy to be mythical. The French are in love with theory and with thin air. The Germans have no vision. I will not set foot in Berlin again until I am as old as Methuselah!" He took Harding's arm, much to the clergy-man's discomfort, and walked with him along the deck. "Only in England do they love Troy. The English believe it will be found. They love warriors."

"They love poets more."

"Nonsense. They are a warrior nation. You will dine with us before we disembark."

Their luncheon, of watery soup and boiled meats, was served in the narrow dining salon on the upper deck. Decimus Harding and the Obermanns sat at one end of a long table, where Obermann was now holding up a bottle. "This, Mr. Harding, is your best English pale ale. I bring it with me everywhere. It is the best cure for constipation known to mankind!" The clergyman glanced at the other passengers. "I was constipated for thirty years, and nothing would move it. Every medicine and potion I tried made it worse, even the famous Carlsberg waters. Then I found English pale ale. I have been trumpeting ever since!"

Harding felt his teeth with his tongue, then swallowed very hard. He was horrified by the volume of Obermann's voice. He glanced quickly at Sophia. She sat looking out to sea, taking care to appear unmoved.

"You see, Harding, it is called Truman's. Now I am a true man!" He leaned over to his wife and brushed a fleck of soot from her embroidered jacket. "Am I not, Frau Obermann?"

The clergyman looked down at his plate, on which he had left the remains of some meat and some oily *pommes frites*. "You were asking me, Herr Obermann, about Frederick Pottle." Ever since Obermann had discovered that Decimus Harding was a clergyman of Oxford he had been questioning him about the various professors and scholars of that university.

"Pottle has always been my enemy," Obermann replied. "He would burn me, stab me, crucify me, anything at all. He utterly refuses to believe that Hissarlik is the site of Homer's Troy, when it is obvious to any man of sense."

"Pottle, my dear sir, is quite mad." Decimus Harding shifted in his seat. This was the kind of conversation he understood and enjoyed. "I have heard that he has been consigned to a lunatic asylum for the last several months."

"Excellent! It is where he belongs."

"He believes himself to be a steam-pump." To his colleagues Decimus Harding was known to be an incorrigible, and quite unreliable, teller of stories. But with his low distinguished voice, and his height, he seemed to Obermann to be the essence of an English gentleman. "Apparently he is in danger of blowing up." Harding had a slight drawl that he used to great effect.

"This is what happens to all of my enemies. Pottle has written a pamphlet, suggesting that the Homeric poems are situated at Bournabashi. It is incredible! Immediately I rebutted his argument point by point, but he was so foolish as to give a lecture on the subject. A steam-pump, you say?" Harding nodded. In fact, at that moment, Frederick Pottle was showing a party of young ladies from the Roehampton Literary Institute around the chapel of Oriel College. "And tell me now of Aspinall. He is still Keeper of Antiquities?"

"Poor Aspinall is drinking, my dear sir. He is a very disappointed man." Harding looked at Obermann, his eyes glittering. "He had to be escorted out of the Ashmolean."

"I am sorry to hear it. He spoke to me of an honorary doctorate."

"I am sorry for his poor wife. She finds him lying on the threshold. Insensible."

"Marriage can be a dangerous business. Is that not so, Sophia?"

She was still gazing out at the Aegean, considering once more the indefinite form that her future had taken. She had always known that she would be married eventually—that was her parents' wish—but she never dreamed that she would be sailing away from Greece with a German husband who spoke in public about his bowels. She could see now that the *Zeus* was coming into harbour; the cries of the seagulls were mixed with the whistles and the blare of the steamer's funnels. Obermann jumped up from the table and bowed to Decimus Harding. "You are going on to Constantinople, Reverend? Very good. As soon as you arrive, you must visit the museum. Give my respects

to Ahmed Nedin, the curator of antiquities. He is a first-rate chap."
He gave the phrase an English pronunciation. "Come, Sophia. We
must supervise the luggage." With his wife following, he strode out of
the narrow salon. Decimus Harding watched them leave with the
strangest smile of triumph.

THREE

"Herr Professor! Professor Obermann!" A young man, who seemed to Sophia to be Slavic in appearance, was waving from the wooden landing-stage of Kannakale.

Obermann raised his right arm above his head. "They like to call me 'Professor.' I see no harm in it."

"Are you not a professor?"

"I have no formal title. I am a professor by deeds, not by words. Come. The gangway is being lowered."

Their luggage was carried before them by four of the ship's porters, bowed low by the weight of boxes and valises, while all around Sophia could smell the atmosphere of an unfamiliar country. The port had the savour of spices, and of goats, but she sensed something else. She was vulnerable here. This was a place that might do her harm. The other passengers, disembarking, were surrounded by porters and by sellers of almond-nuts and pomegranates and dried frogs; they screamed and shouted in what was for Sophia an unintelligible language. But they seemed to know, or recognise, her husband; they held back as the young man who had hailed him made his way through the crowd.

"Well met, Telemachus. May I have the honour of introducing you to Frau Obermann?"

The young man bowed, but when she held out her hand to him, he put it up to his lips without kissing it. She sensed that he distrusted, or disliked, her. How could that be?

"Where are your manners, Telemachus? Frau Obermann is our Greek deity now. She has come to claim back her old city!"

"No, Heinrich." For some reason the sentiment alarmed her. "I am only your wife."

"Do you hear the modesty of the Greek woman, Telemachus? The husband, be he old or young, is everything to her. Heaven and earth have a secondary interest! Where is our cart?"

She had not expected this. The luggage was hauled by Telemachus on to the back of an ancient wagon that might have been taken from a farmyard; its wheels had no spokes, but were made of solid discs of wood carved into shape. Obermann helped her into the vehicle where two planks, running cross-wise and covered by rugs, were used as seats or benches. At the bottom of the cart she saw traces of straw and dung. "I would have ordered you a golden chariot, Sophia, but they are all occupied at the moment." The driver wore the peculiar fez of the region, the base wrapped in white linen, and Sophia noticed that the rim of linen was stained with the marks of sweat. He prodded the two horses with a tapering stick, and they began their slow journey through the narrow streets of Kannakale. She sat beside her husband, who was smiling broadly and taking off his white Panama hat to greet various shopkeepers whom they passed. Three children ran after the cart calling, "*Hakim! Hakim!*"

"What are they saying, Heinrich?"

"I am a great doctor to them on the plain. I have a large medicine box for any conceivable sickness, so they come to me. I cure them."

"I did not know that you were trained in medicine."

"Trained? Of course not. It is what the English call 'common sense.' I see a child with fever. I give him two drops of quinine. I see anaemia, and I prescribe the iron powder. I see vomiting, and I give them chalk and laudanum. They have none of our European diseases

THE FALL OF TROY

such as measles. They lead healthy lives, like their ancestors. I cannot find the old plane tree under which the father of medicine received the sick. I am not Hippocrates. But I work upon the same people."

"Are you not afraid of spreading European disease?"

"Me? Nonsense! I am the healthiest man on earth! Good day to you, sir!" He lifted his hat to a man dressed in a Western suit. "And, besides, my patients bring me gifts. They bring me coins and vases taken out of the soil. I am a magnet. I attract the finds!" He seemed to lose himself in contemplation.

Telemachus was sitting at the front of the cart, beside the driver, and Sophia leaned forward to tap him on the shoulder. "You are Greek?"

"Me? Oh, no, Madame. I am from St. Petersburg." He still evinced the same curious coldness.

"But your name is Greek."

"Telemachus is the name the professor has given to me. My real name is Leonid. Leonid Pluyshin."

"He is the son of a colleague I left in Russia," Obermann said. "He is a wily banker, and so I called his son Telemachus."

Obermann had worked as a merchant in St. Petersburg for seven years; he had principally traded in indigo and saltpetre, which, in the unsettled conditions of the time, had provided him with a substantial fortune. He had then invested that fortune in property, in Berlin and in Paris, and had acquired a large stake in the railways of Cuba.

They had left the town of Kannakale and had come on to a dusty road, stony and uneven, with ruts and scars across it. "There are no true roads in this region," Obermann said. "We are back in the Bronze Age." On either side of them were fields of long grass, flow-ing like the waves of the sea, and Sophia could feel the wind on her back coming from the north. "It is always windy here," he said. "I find it exciting. I find purpose in it! That is what Homer calls it. Windy Troy. The same wind blows through history, Sophia. Do you not feel it?" He turned around in the cart, and put his face to the rushing air. "In the fifth book of the *Iliad* the poet sings of the north wind. Boreas. It sweeps down from the mountain tops and scatters the shadowy clouds. It is proof that Homer came to this place." They crossed a stone bridge, over a little stream, and all Sophia could hear now was the chinking of the horses' bells and the occasional bleating of goats. "Look west, Sophia, towards the sea. Do you see those two small hills close by the shore?" She could see two mounds, covered with bushes and trees; with the light of the sea behind them, they seemed to glimmer close to the horizon. "They are supposed by the people to be the tombs of Patroclus and Achilles. The two male lovers lying side by side! And yet they punish sodomy with death! We will enter those tombs, Telemachus. I wish to look upon the face of Achilles. *Palai katatethnotos.* You understand that, Sophia?"

"One who died long ago."

"The language of your ancestors is close to you. This is what we will do. We will recite long passages from Homer, and we will learn them by heart. We will memorise them." The dusty track had narrowed as they came upon the plain of Troy. "Welcome to the meadows of Asia, Sophia!"

All around her now she saw the tall grasses, which seemed to be growing out of marshland, while, beyond them, there were fields studded with red and yellow flowers. The flat land stretched towards the sea, to the west, while to the east it gave way to ridges and distant mountains of which the higher peaks were covered with snow. There seemed to be oak trees growing all over this plain, hunched over in the direction of the wind like dark pygmies. Obermann turned to her and pointed out some small houses by the side of the track. "You know it is spring here, Sophia, when the storks nest upon the flat roofs. Do you see them?" She saw the untidy baskets of twigs and reeds. "This is the season when they return."

They had followed the track by the side of a river tangled with overgrowth and trees. Sophia could see rushes growing beside its banks, and for a moment she sensed the comfort of a green haven away from the dust and the wind. There was a series of small islands, in the middle of the river, covered with willows and elms. "The Scamander," Obermann said to her. "That is the language of man. In the language of the gods this river is known as Xanthus, or the yellow stream. It is curious that rivers all over the world preserve their names with wonderful persistency. Homer called it *dineis,* eddying, or *dios,* divine. It was said to have been born of Zeus and was venerated by the people as a god. It had its own priest in Troy. Does that seem strange to you? It is not strange at all. We will follow its course until it meets the Simois. See how it flows! Hector called his son Scamandrus." He seemed changed by the landscape around him. He was no longer in the society of men, but in the company of gods. That was how she put it to herself. "Water is the oldest thing upon the earth," he was saying. "But it is ageless. Ever fresh and ever renewed."

Sophia suddenly felt very hungry, and took from her cloth-bag a packet of small chocolate cakes. She offered one to her husband. He took the packet, and crammed several into his mouth. She was about to pass the confection to the driver, but Obermann stopped her. "Never offer gifts to a Turk. He cannot refuse. And he would be obliged to return the favour."

"That does not apply to a Russian, I take it?"

"Nothing applies to Telemachus. But he does not like to eat sweet things. He consumes vast quantities of meat, like a lion, but he cannot touch one particle of sugar. Is that not so, Telemachus?" The young man laughed out loud. "You see? He laughs at his own weakness. That is the Russian way." Obermann leaned forward, and tapped him on the shoulder. "When you die I will erect a tumulus for you on the plain. The tomb of Telemachus."

"You will outlive me then, Professor?"

"Oh, yes. I am ageless. Beside, I have a young bride." The driver suddenly pointed his stick across the plain, and seemed to sing out two notes. "Look there, do you see, Sophia? A wolf!" She glimpsed some dark-haired animal, running among the grasses and the trees, and felt curiously happy.

"A beauty!" Obermann was exultant. "He comes from Mount Ida. The mother of wild beasts. See how he streaks across the earth. The plain is welcoming you, Sophia. It is showing you its delights. Soon you will have thunder from Zeus, and all will be perfect."

"It is good luck to see a wolf," she replied, "in my country. Not in packs, of course. But a single wolf is a good omen."

"Did you hear that, Telemachus? The gods are auspicious."

They travelled in silence for a while, as the track diverged from the bank of the Scamander and passed through what appeared to be swampy ground; and then they came upon a terrain of small hills covered with oaks, low shrubs and bushes.

"We are approaching," Obermann said, "the *mysterium tremendum*."

She could hear the river again, rushing through the masses of trees lining its banks. They crossed another roughly hewn stone bridge and came to the outskirts of a small village with its houses of thatch and mud-brick. And then she saw the hill. Or, rather, it was not a hill but a great outcrop of rock and mud at the very end of a ridge. Yet it also resembled a castle, with defensive ramparts and earthen towers. They rode through the narrow street of the village, watched by several women and children, and approached the mound.

"Welcome to Troy," her husband said. "Every city that ever was and every city that ever will be." It rose above them and, as they came closer, she could see people working upon it; it was teeming with life, like some nest or burrow. It was a living thing. "In the language of the gods it is called Ilium. It is the most famous place on the whole earth."

The cart stopped, and Leonid helped her to dismount as Obermann strode in the direction of the mound. He had taken off his hat, and was surveying the scene; his arms were stretched out, and he cried aloud some words in Turkish.

"He is greeting his workers," Leonid said. "He has missed them greatly."

Sophia did not wish to approach the mound yet. "It is built upon this hill?"

"No. It is not a hill. It is not a natural object at all. It is made by man." As he spoke about Troy his reserve towards her seemed to lighten. He sensed, perhaps, her excitement. "These are all the levels of the city. For thousands of years each version of the city was built on top of its predecessor. What you see are the layers of a cake. A human cake."

"And these rocks?"

"Not rocks but stones. Stone walls. Stone roads. The earth is the mud-brick of the houses, fallen into ruin. The professor believes it to be the first and most ancient city. He calls it Troy but to the people here it is known as Hissarlik. That is their word for a fortress hill."

"If it were a beast, it would move one to pity."

"Pity, yes, and terror. Awe. I never see it without wishing to bow my head."

She looked more carefully now. There were several steep slopes, which had the appearance of ramparts, but the central area was flattened into a plateau where numerous remains of stone walls were visible. She could see workmen trundling wheelbarrows on makeshift tracks, and there were women carrying baskets upon their heads. Other men had pickaxes and shovels. They were clambering over the sides of the mound. It was a scene of intense activity, in the middle of this drowsy plain.

She went over to her husband, who was standing in the shade of a solitary fig tree, mopping his brow with a cotton handkerchief. "I am opening a new world. Sophia! Come with me. This is your home." He took her hand and led her across the grass and loose earth towards Hissarlik. There was a shallow slope on the north side where a narrow trackway had been formed between deep trenches; all around her there seemed to be ditches, depressions and small hills. He noticed her glance. "Yes. It is like a scene of battle," he said. "We are the warriors beating on the gates."

"Who are all these people, Heinrich?"

"Mainly Turks. A few Greeks and Asiatic Jews. I curse them in their own languages. The Turks work better than the Greeks. Forgive me for saying so, Sophia, but they are more honest. And they work on Sundays, which no Greek will ever do."

"It is a holy day, Heinrich."

"Every day on Troy is a holy day. It is a sacred place. A shrine." He paused, bent down, and picked up a piece of pottery; he cleaned it with his thumb, looked at it keenly, then threw it back on to the earth. "It was here that Asia and Europe, East and West, first met in conflict. It is here that literature began. Does that not make it holy?"

They walked further up the slope, and she felt more keenly the strong wind. "What was that piece you threw down?"

"Roman. Nothing more. The whole site is awash with fragments of pottery."

"Is not the Roman very ancient?"

"If we were looking for Hellenistic Ilium it would be profitable. But we are not. Look down there." He pointed to what seemed to be a newly dug shaft. "Do you see how far it is gone? It is like a funnel. At the bottom of the funnel will be the most ancient Troy. The first city." For some reason she had a vision of a whirlpool, not a funnel, and within its rushing vortex lay an ancient place.

"How far down, Heinrich?" She peered into the darkness.

"Thirty or forty feet. It is impossible to say. Archaeology is not something you can learn at university. It is not cut and dried. I have found levels of Roman occupation here and, below them, the Stone Age! For a moment my mind is deranged. How could the Stone Age live on into the time of the Empire? But then a theory presents itself. My honoured colleague Professor Lineau tells me that this part of the site was not used for thousands of years. The Romans found an area of unused stone, and built upon it. All becomes clear! You will meet Lineau very soon. I found him at the Sorbonne."

Sophia did not particularly wish to meet anyone else that afternoon: she was too bewildered by her early sensations, too distracted by the noise and activity around her, to keep command of herself. She longed for rest and quietness.

"When I first arrived here," Obermann was saying, "I had only one workman. Only one! I gave him a spade, and told him to dig. What did he find but a little wooden idol? Here. I keep it with me always, for the good luck it brings." He took from his pocket a small carved figure with a mouth shaped like an O. "It calls to me, saying, 'Go on! Go on!'" He put it back in his pocket, and patted it. "Now I have one hundred and fifty men and women. Each one earns nine piastres per day. If they come to see me with an especial find, I pay them a bonus of twenty-five piastres. Nothing can escape a Turk's eye when he is looking for a bonus! It is a small expense, but the gain in antiquities is immense."

The wind had picked up more strength, and there was a chill in the afternoon air. And then she saw three workmen carrying her luggage, on their backs, up the slope of Hissarlik. "What are these men doing, Heinrich?"

"They are taking our cases to our house. I told you this was your new home, did I not?"

"What? We are living here?"

"Of course. Where else are we supposed to live, Sophia? The houses on the plain are filled with vermin. Here we are free of bed-bugs." She had expected them to be lodged in the village they had passed, or even in the port of Kannakale, but to live upon a dirt hill— was that possible? "Why look so afraid, Sophia? That is why I married a young wife. You are strong. You must get used to adventure! Do you see here? These are the walls of a palace. Do you see? You will be living in a palace!" There were women formed in a line, taking away earth in what appeared to be dough-baskets. They were chanting some Turkish song in low voices. The men were in a trench with pickaxes, cutting away the ridges of dark earth from which the walls were emerging. They had wound shawls around their faces, to protect them from the dust and wind, so that they looked to her like muffled mourners at an Ottoman funeral. All this was to be her home.

"My shoes slip in the mud, Heinrich."

"Only a little further." And then they came upon the plateau on top of the mound. There were more trenches and ridges here, but there was also a range of stone and wooden huts. "Welcome to Ober-mannopolis," he said. "You are its queen." He laughed out loud, star-tling her. "Except, I forgot, it is a republic." He led her towards a stone hut surrounded by deep trenches. "This is where we live."

When she entered, cautiously, she found herself in a large room with a bed at one end and a rudimentary kitchen and hearth at the other. The floor, of beaten earth, was covered with rush-mats and Turkey carpets. "It was built with stones from Ilium, Sophia. We live in primitive comfort." Their luggage had been deposited on the floor, and she sat down upon one of the cases. "The walls are two feet thick." She would not cry in front of him. She had promised him, in Athens, that she would never cry again. Yet in Athens he had told her that she would have good and comfortable lodgings and that, after a short stay in Troy, he would take her on a journey to Paris and to London. She noticed that the ceiling was made of planks covered with rough thatch. "The roof is covered with waterproof felt," he said. He seemed always to know what she was thinking. "We are snug." He was still watching her keenly—she knew that—and she was determined to betray no feeling. "You had not expected this, Sophia?"

"I expected nothing. I did not know what to expect. As you said before, I am young."

"Do you have the jewels you brought from Athens?"

"They are safe."

"I will show you a place to hide them. Not everyone is to be trusted."

Someone called to him, and he went out of the stone hut. As soon as he had left her, she put her face into her hands and wept.

FOUR

She could not sleep. She could hear the north wind whistling
through the crevices in the old stones. And she could hear the
owls, myriads of owls, calling to the night. He had warned her
of their noise. He said that they nested in the holes of the trenches,
but she wondered how that could be. It was yet another mystery. He
had confessed at supper that evening that he found their clamour and
their hooting disturbing; he had described it as a hideous shrieking.
But the noise somehow soothed her; the owls had sounded sympathetic to her fate. He had told her, too, that the thousands of frogs in
the swamps and marshes would join in the chorus.

She left the bed as quietly as she could, with her husband sleeping
silently beside her. Her eyes were already accustomed to the darkness.
She put on her bed-coat, which she had draped over a simple wooden
chair, and found her night-shoes. When she opened the door of the
hut she felt the wind envelop her. It overwhelmed her. It seemed to
her to occupy, not to haunt, this place. It would always be here. She
made her way carefully along a path between the trenches that led di-
rectly to the old palace walls. In the light of the moon they appeared
newly built. And, when she looked up, she had never seen the stars so
clearly. She searched for, and quickly found, the constellation of Ursa

Major. It seemed so close that she might put up her hand and touch it. She followed its arc across the sky and found the bright star, Arcturus, in the constellation of the Boötes. She murmured the words she had learned as a child, when she and her nurse had sat in the garden in the evening before she was lifted up and carried in to her bed. *Aspetos aither.* The pure sky. Now, when she looked across Hissarlik, she could sense the shape of old Troy all around her. For the first time since her arrival she understood its form. Earlier, before supper, Heinrich had explained to her the alignment of the palace with the main street leading to the great Scaian gate; he had drawn on some paper the circuit of the walls around the ancient city, and the extent of the houses and gardens stretching beyond those walls. Now, in the night and darkness, Troy was visible.

Mother of God. Someone was sitting upon a rock just ahead of her, his body hunched over. She must have spoken out loud because the man arose and removed his hat. "Frau Obermann? Forgive me. I am lost in my thoughts." He spoke in English to her. "My name is Lineau." She was immediately aware of the impropriety. She was dressed only in her nightgown and coat. But when she saw the milky white orbs of his eyes, she realised that he was blind. "I am sorry to have missed you at dinner, Frau Obermann. I was visiting a rogue who deals in antiquities."

"My husband has told me of you."

"Yes, I am the French professor with the mad theories! That is why I sit at night and smoke my pipe."

It was Lineau's belief that Troy had been built upon the site of a holy place, a shrine of a god or a tomb of some great king, and that the original inhabitants were priests or guardians of the sacred spot. He believed that in some manner, also, the position of the city upon the plain was aligned with the movement of the stars. That was why Homer celebrated it in the *Iliad,* and why it had been fought over so fiercely.

"I have grown accustomed to the owls," he said. "The goddess of Troy, Athene, is known as *glaucopis,* or owl-eyed. Why should they not inhabit this place? This is where they belong."

"In my country they are considered birds of death."

"Precisely. This is a place of death, is it not? What are we doing here but calling back the dead? It is the bird of night. It sat on the spear of Pyrrhus when he advanced against Argos. I have found a tomb in Ionia where two owls sit on the left and right of a siren, the songstress of the death-wail. Has Herr Obermann not told you of the vases we have found here, which are decorated with owls' faces? They are unique to Troy. This is the place of death and night."

She was enveloped by the wind once more, and strained to catch his words. You see nothing, she thought, and you see everything.

In fact Lineau's blindness had not affected his passion for archaeology. He took no part in the digging, but he had an unrivalled reputation for the recognition and identification of finds. From the texture of a fragment of vase he could determine the period in which it had been used; from the loop of a handle, or the rim of a broken dish, he could reconstruct the entire shape of the piece. He knew the provenance, and the variety, of each item laid before him; he could trace the delicate lines where a figure or pattern had been inscribed upon the surface.

"Your husband used to read Homer to me each evening," he said. "I have missed him."

"I detained him in Athens too long, I expect. Forgive me."

"There is nothing to forgive. You are young and, from your voice, I judge you to be beautiful." She laughed. But then there was a movement somewhere on the side of the mound. "The Turkish guard," he said. "Villagers come here searching for gold."

"Do they find it?"

"We cannot be sure. Something hidden from us by chance—something overlooked. It is possible. The wind is blowing too hard for you, I think." She had not realised that she was shivering. "Let me escort you to your little house." He led the way up the track towards the plateau. "You must beware of centipedes, Frau Obermann. I think of them as their names, little Latin animals. In Greece, I believe, you call them *sarantopodia*."

"Yes. With forty feet."

"And forty mouths. They have a deadly bite. You must sweep your ceiling every night." She shuddered. "Let me show you something. It will make you less fearful. Over here." He led her down a portion of the slope, just beyond the walls of the palace, where there was a small circular construction of stone. "Do you see it, Frau Obermann? I believe that here was the shrine of their god. Its image was kept in a wooden box."

"It was Zeus?"

"Zeus. The lord of the dark clouds. The shaker of the earth. He had a thousand names. Be quiet, if you please. The god is still here." They stood in silence for a while, with the calling of the owls all around them, and then he touched her arm. "I will take you back now."

―⁓―

WHEN SHE AWOKE, the following morning, Obermann was nowhere to be seen. She boiled some coffee on the Franklin stove, tucked away in a corner of the alcove used as the kitchen, and as she sipped it she noticed with some surprise that her mood had altogether changed. She no longer felt the weariness she had first experienced when she had toiled up the slope of Hissarlik. She no longer felt desolate. The god was still here.

She left the hut, and saw her husband standing on one of the mounds like a conqueror, calling out to various workers and pointing with his ebony cane. "Go there with your spade! Do you see that curve in the wall? Dig! Dig!" He caught sight of his wife, and turned to greet her. "While you slept, Sophia, I have ridden down to the sea and bathed. I am refreshed. I have conversed with Poseidon! He said to me, 'My dear Obermann, your wife should be with you.'"

"I am sorry, Heinrich. Our journey tired me."

"You cannot be tired here, dear Sophia. We are in the first days of the world. Demetriou!" he called, to one of the workmen. "What is that depression there? Is it a pit?"

She did indeed feel strangely exhilarated. She was looking north over the Trojan plain towards the Dardanelles and the Hellespont, but when she turned, she could see the peaks of the Ida mountains covered with snow. On the other side was the coastline, the sea and the distant island of Tenedos. It occurred to her that there were in nature only curved lines, like the slopes of the hill on which she was standing, and that all was in unison. She watched the men and women, bent over to dig into the soil: they were digging simultaneously in several places, and she noticed that they had acquired a continual and consistent rhythm of working.

"You see, Sophia, it is like a child being raised from the dead. My child! It has come to life after thirty-one centuries. Now here comes my nemesis. He is our Turkish overseer. A monster. Good morning to you, Kadri Bey." Obermann made a flicker of his fingers from belly to breast to forehead; at the same time he bowed, a gesture reciprocated by the official, who was dressed in a kaftan of white cloth with an embroidered leathern girdle in the approved Constantinople style. "You see that Frau Obermann has joined our little band."

Kadri Bey bowed and again touched his chest. "Welcome, welcome. We are honoured." She noticed that his eyes were very bright. "This is a land of treasures, Frau Obermann, as you can see."

"We are not interested in treasure, Kadri Bey. We are interested in history."

"Of course, Herr Obermann. But the ladies love treasures."

"I do not love treasures," Sophia said. She observed that a curved dagger was attached to his girdle.

"May I show your wife something?"

"Of course."

Kadri Bey led her across the plateau among the carts and the wagons. "English wheelbarrows," he said. "Iron wheels. Very good." He picked up a hoe. "In Turkish we call this *eschapa*. But this is not what I show you." They walked over to a low wall, against which two men were kneeling and cutting away the earth with short knives. "Do you see the fragments all around here?" She nodded; she could see small pieces of baked clay and bone. "Ancient pottery. But there is something else." He muttered to one of the workmen, who took from the pocket of his canvas waistcoat a linen cloth; within it was wrapped what looked to Sophia like gold wire clotted with dark soil. "Rings for the ears," Kadri Bey said. "A lady wore them once." His eyes glittered as he spoke to her.

She smiled and turned away, walking across the plateau to rejoin her husband. "Do you like our Turk?" he asked her.

"I do not know him."

"It is said that the Turk hates the Christian, but he is the worst of all. His conceit is boundless. His knowledge is nothing. And I am obliged to pay him fifteen pounds a month in English sterling for the privilege of his company! He is sent here by the Turkish government to spy on me. That is all."

"To spy?"

"They do not trust me. He instructs his workmen to give him the finds, which he notes down before presenting them to me. The Turks believe that I will make them disappear into thin air." He laughed. "And of course I will. Troy is not for Turkey. Troy is for the world. What was it that he showed you?" She had had no idea that he had been watching her.

"An ornament, I think. Gold wire."

"He exults in these small things. He is a shopkeeper. I will share a secret with my wife. Already I have found a greater object by far. It is hidden from him." Kadri Bey was walking towards them. "I was saying, Kadri Bey, that you have the eyes of an eagle."

"Perhaps I need them, Herr Obermann."

"I also have those eyes. Before we sank the shaft, I considered it certain that we should find remnants of primeval Troy. You saw it yesterday, Sophia. I knew it to be there. But you doubted it, Kadri Bey. You raised your hands to God. I paid no attention."

"You are an infidel, Herr Obermann."

"On the contrary. *Semper fidelis.* Faithful to Troy." He turned to Sophia. "We worked during the first two days with picks and shovels, but the next two days we had to employ baskets. I filled them myself with the debris and carried them away from the shaft, such was my confidence. When we reached the depth of thirteen feet, I was obliged to erect a wooden triangle, and draw up the baskets with windlasses."

"The heat was very great," Kadri Bey said. "Too great for the workmen."

"I know it. I was in the depths. And the atmosphere grew foul with the petroleum lamps. But I insisted that we continue. The soil at those depths was as hard as stone, but we dug. And what did we find, Kadri Bey?"

"Some stones."

"More than stones. A work of giants. There were, Sophia, the stones of a great monument! What little we can see leaves no doubt in my mind that it was of vast dimensions and that it was executed with consummate art. That night we drank thirty-two and a half bottles of Greek wine and roasted two sheep. It was a great feast, Telemachus, was it not?"

Leonid had come up to them quietly.

"I am going into the village for provisions," he said. "With your permission, Herr Professor, I wonder if your wife would like to see our neighbours?"

"Of course. She would be delighted. Is that not so, Sophia?"

"I will be happy to accompany you, Leonid." She sensed that he was beginning to enjoy her company. He had relented. "If you wait, I will find my hat and parasol."

"Hat? You have no need of a hat, Sophia. We are not in the nineteenth century. We are in Troy."

"I must find my hat, Heinrich."

"Pooh." She stared at him, and was surprised by her own resolution. "Very well. So be it. Have your hat."

When she came up to the horse and cart, with her hat firmly in place, she was elated. "Do let us go another way from yesterday," she said to Leonid. "I will see more of the plain." So he gave instructions to the driver, a younger man than the day before, and they rode out into the lush land beyond the marshes where sheep and long-horned cattle were being watched by peasant boys. There was a track here, used by the villagers.

"My husband does not care for Kadri Bey," she said.

"Kadri? He is not a bad man. He is devoted to the interests of his country. That is all."

"Are the interests of my husband so very different?"

"You husband's interests are—are mysterious." He laughed. "Forgive me, Frau Obermann. I should not be talking to you like this."

"Oh, no. Go on. I will say nothing of this to anyone."

He glanced at her, as she sat upright upon the bench. "Your husband has many interests. When we first came here he pointed out to me some verses from the *Iliad,* where Homer describes the treasure-chamber of Priam. I do not know if you have studied the passage?" She shook her head. "It is vaulted, with a high roof. It is fragrant with cedarwood and contains many splendid jewels. Your husband truly believes that the chamber is somewhere beneath our feet. That is why he is so eager to dig in every place. And as for the jewels—"

"Yes?"

"He would like to see them, I believe."

"And he would not give them to Kadri Bey?"

"I think not." He glanced at her again. "This is where you may misunderstand me, Frau Obermann. The professor has a genuine passion for discovery. He searches for Troy like a lover. He will not leave here until he has uncovered the old city and disclosed it to the world. It is his life. He believes every word of Homer to be true."

"As you say, he is mysterious."

She was about to mention the object that her husband had admitted having concealed, but decided to say nothing. They sat in silence as they came up to the village of Chiplak. It comprised no more than a road of beaten earth, with thatched dwellings on either side of it. "They live like their ancestors," Leonid said. "Their houses are the same. Do you see? The ground floor is for storage." Sophia observed that the ground floors were of unwrought stone without doors or windows. Above them was a floor walled with clay bricks. Each house seemed to have a courtyard or garden behind it, also walled with clay. "They build them out of the earth and mud around them," he said. "Fortunately it does not rain very much in the Troad."

"They are like little castles."

"The wind. They keep it at bay."

"And what happens when the rain comes?"

"Oh, it is ferocious. It drives in from the sea. It washes away the roofs. And then the walls. Nothing is left standing except these stone foundations. Then they look very like the ruins of Hissarlik." They had come up to one end of the village, where two mules were tethered to a post. "Here I go to see the woman. She sells the bread and the fruit."

When he came out of the small yard with the driver, both of them carrying sacks of produce, Sophia was nowhere to be seen. They called out for her several times, and eventually she emerged from a narrow track that led off the main path. "I have found a mound like a grave," she said, "covered in herbs and flowers. Beside it is a spring and a wild fig tree. It is enchanting."

"In the field? It is a shrine. A farmer found there—what do you call it—an ammonite. An ancient fossil of the sea. It is curled like the horn of a ram, and the villagers believe it to be the relic of some legendary beast. They consider it sacred. It hangs in the farmer's house now, with little bells draped around it. Then, by some stroke of great good fortune, that spring was discovered beside it. So now they venerate the spot."

"The sea covered this plain?"

"Oh, indeed. We have found literally millions of sea-shells on Hissarlik alone. I said to the professor that we had discovered Atlantis."

———~~~———

THEY ALL DINED together that evening, Lineau and Kadri Bey, Leonid and the Obermanns, and their conversation had turned to the trees mentioned in Homer. "It is called *phegos*," Lineau was saying to the Turkish overseer. "But who knows what is meant by this?"

"Our tree here is the oak, Monsieur Lineau."

"But you also have beech in abundance."

"That is so."

"It was a high tree and sacred to Zeus." Obermann had scarcely been listening to them. "On this *phegos* Athene and Apollo sat in the shape of vultures, to enjoy the sight of the battle." He took a large bite from a slice of pickled tongue. "Does that not stir the blood? That is why I forbid the cutting down of any trees."

"Homer mentions one particular tree, Professor." Leonid had been studying the *Iliad,* in Russian translation, ever since his arrival in Hissarlik. "It was by the great gates of the city."

"*Ja, ja.* Yes, of course I know this. It was the tree where Apollo clothed himself in mist and fog, secretly to encourage Antenor. It is the tree in whose shade wounded Sarpedon lay."

"Here you have white beech." Lineau was still addressing Kadri Bey. "In my country we have red beech. It is the smaller tree."

"What does that signify?" Obermann turned his attention to that end of the table. "It is known to the world that the Homeric tree is the oak. Pliny says so emphatically. *Quercus.* They were known for their great age in his time. Is that not good enough for you?"

"Yet it might be the chestnut, Professor." Leonid enjoyed the company of Obermann when he grew excited or indignant.

"The chestnut? What does the chestnut have to do with anything?"

"It has been mentioned. That is all."

"Mentioned? Anything can be mentioned. It proves nothing."

Sophia had quietly left the table. They were dining in the wooden, barrack-like hut that was used as a store-house for the antiquities found at Hissarlik. It was also the place where the pickaxes, wooden shovels, and other tools were kept overnight. She picked up a small bowl from the vessels that had yet to be examined and labelled; it had a curious band of marks or shapes around its rim, discoloured and obscured by earth. There was a small knife among the tools, and she sat down upon a stool in order to clean the vessel of its detritus. The shapes upon the rim became visible: a cross, or a wheel, it was difficult to tell. Could it be a cross and a wheel combined? It seemed to Sophia that she was allowing the bowl to speak. It had been imprisoned in the earth for thousands of years, but now had come back into the light. What Trojan woman last saw it—last used it, for milk or honey? She would have placed her hands just so, as Sophia placed hers around it. There was a union between them, one living and one dead.

"You have an instinct, Sophia. I see it very clearly." Obermann had been watching her, as she sat absorbed in the task. "You used the knife with care. My wife is already an archaeologist, gentlemen. She needs no education. I am the same. I became an archaeologist when I set out to find the palace of Odysseus. I landed on Ithaca, and I found it. I climbed Mount Aetos, and I dug. That is archaeology. Instinct!"

FIVE

These mornings of late spring were still cold. Sophia was wrapped in a shawl as she dug into the recently exposed soil on the southern slope of Hissarlik. She was leading a group of workmen who sang in unison as they cleared away the earth and debris; they had been employed on this part of Hissarlik for two days, and Obermann had already discerned the shape of a temple or a dwelling. He had seen nothing in particular but, as he had said to Sophia, "My imagination is correct."

She had already proved herself to be a rapid and eager student. He had taught her how to remove the earth methodically, how to identify the salient points in any trench or pit, how to recognise and remove any significant finds without damaging them. "It is not a science," he had said. "It is an art."

Lineau explained to her the various ages of the artefacts to be found at Troy, and how to distinguish between them in shape and appearance. There were two-handled amphorae, unique to this place, which were of the third century before Christ; there were bronze vessels of the sixth century B.C.; there was black pottery of the eighth century B.C. There were whorls and whetstones from as early as the tenth century before Christ, as well as terracotta balls and vases from earliest antiquity. All of these things she studied and remembered.

She learned other things. "If you find anything of value," Obermann said to her, "it must become invisible."

"Of value, Heinrich?"

"Precious metals. Jewels. There is much gold to be found here. But it must be hidden from Kadri Bey. I do not want the glories of Troy to be given to Turkey. Shall I tell you where they are going? To Athens. To your native *polis*." He lowered his voice, although no one was near them. "I have come to an agreement with your father. He has found me a house close to your own. I use that as my store-room. Once a week a Greek workman takes the valuables in saddle-bags to the steamer. Then he sails to Athens, where your father meets him. It is so safe. So simple."

Sophia was taken aback. It seemed that Heinrich had been negotiating with her father on other matters, while wooing her at home.

—∿∿—

THE NEXT MORNING, just before dawn, Obermann roused her and led her from their bed. In the alcove that served as a kitchen, he carefully took up three floorboards—there, concealed beneath the boards, was a shallow wooden box half filled with goblets and pendants and other pieces of glinting metal. "Here is a brooch of gold and ivory," he said. "It may have been worn by Helen herself. Here is a vase-cover of electrum. And here a spoon of silver, with a large omphalos in the middle. All of them priceless, Sophia! Do you feel the presence of Andromache and Hecuba? These were the jewels they wore in well-walled Troy!" He put back the floorboards. "I cannot announce their discovery as yet. Not until we have left Turkey behind for ever. But I have made notes of where and when they were found. I have become one of those *Schematiker*. I have become German! I have been methodical. Did you know that method comes from the Greek, Sophia? *Meta hodos*. Along the path. That is the direction in which I am travelling."

SHE HAD TIED canvas sacking to her legs so that she could kneel on the hard ground: she believed at first that she had found the line of a wall but the stone had curved downwards as she dug away the soil clinging to its rough surface. She was damp with sweat, and for a moment put her face up to the cool wind that came from the direction of the Hellespont. She was cramped, out of breath, and her fingers ached from persistent digging. But she was content to be part of this labour at Troy, part of the song of the workmen.

During the course of the morning one of them came up to her with a small cup, perfectly preserved in the earth, with an ornamentation of zigzag lines. Her husband had warned her that the workers would sometimes incise the lines with their own knives, in order to increase the value of their finds; he had once caught a Turkish labourer forging the decoration of a plate, by creating a solar disc with rays, but Obermann had been so pleased with the addition that he kept it and catalogued it. Sophia had been horrified by his account of this double deception, but he had laughed. "You do not know the moral of this story, Sophia. The man had by chance drawn precisely the symbol used by some of the Trojan potters! It was a miracle. In my opinion the genius of Troy was working through him. It must be preserved for posterity, even if you and I alone know the secret. Of course I still fined him. It sets an example." So by degrees she became accustomed to Obermann's archaeology.

The small cup seemed to her to be genuine, and she gave the Turkish worker ten piastres for bringing it to her. Her own work was proceeding slowly, until she noticed that the stone sloped downwards but then continued out again as a horizontal ledge. She called some men to the site and asked them to dig with shovels and spades on this spot. Within less than an hour they had uncovered three levels of stonework. "Heinrich! Here is a staircase!" she called to him from the top of the trench. "Heinrich! Here!"

He had been standing in a shallow pit, some feet away, and immediately joined her. "Do you see?" she asked him. "These are steps."

"It is as you say." He leaped down into the trench, and examined the stone more closely. "This is wonderful, Sophia. Whenever I see a stairway coming out of the earth, I experience the strangest sensation. I go from earth to air. I am transported. These are Trojan steps!" He stood upon them, and banged his heels upon their pitted surface. "We must dig deeper. Always deeper."

He set eighty men to dig through the ground lying around the stairway, and by the evening they had partially uncovered a large building which, to Obermann's evident delight, had been destroyed by a terrible fire. The interior was filled with black, red and yellow wood ash and with the charred remains of innumerable objects. Sophia had uncovered an area of the city previously unknown. "We must call it the Sophia district," he said. But the idea horrified her.

"I am certain of what happened here," he said that night. They were eating Chicago corned beef with tinned ox-tongues and Turkish cheeses. "These are houses beyond the palace where the families took refuge after the onslaught by the Greeks. Priam is slain at the altar of Athene, which we will find soon enough. His wife, Hecuba, is enslaved to Odysseus. His daughter, Polyxene, is taken off to be sacrificed at the tomb of Achilles. His grandson, Astyanax, is hurled from one of the tall towers of the city. Do you see it, Sophia? Aias rapes Cassandra in the sanctuary of Zeus Heracleion—which Monsieur Lineau to his everlasting glory has located . . ." Lineau put out his hands in a gesture of submission. "Ever afterwards the statue of the god looked towards the sky. All is confusion. So the remnants of the family—Deiphobus and his brothers—flee to the house that my wife has uncovered. There they are ringed with fire. When we have gone deeper, we will find human skeletons. I am sure of it."

Kadri Bey had been watching him intently. "If there is a body, Herr Obermann, there must be a burial. In Turkish law—"

"Troy knows no laws, Kadri Bey."

"If it is the body of a slain warrior, then it must be given due honour."

"He will have more honour in death than he ever had in life. He will be carried in triumph around the world!"

"His grave must be here. On his own soil."

"We have found nothing as yet," Leonid said calmly. "The argument has no meaning. Can I mention another matter before you all? A workman has told me that two of the women in the village are wearing strange jewels of spun gold. They were boasting to the other women that they possessed them, and last night they had the effrontery to wear them. You know where they come from, I take it?"

Obermann laughed very loudly. "Their husbands have found them here and kept them. It is monstrous! You must get them back, Telemachus, and scold the women for their impertinence."

"And their husbands?"

"They must have sharp eyes. Fine them. But keep them on. I need such men."

"No, Herr Obermann." Kadri Bey was carefully dividing a tinned American peach. "If this is theft, then the authorities at Kannakale must be informed. Otherwise there will be no end of robbery."

"So be it."

"It is just."

"I bow to you in this matter, Kadri Bey. You are quite right. Theft must not be rewarded."

Sophia did not look at her husband and, instead, turned to Lineau with a question. Had he examined the vase that Heinrich had found the day before, by the wall of the palace? She had noticed that it had the same strange marks—the cross or wheel—she had seen on a cup that morning.

"It is not altogether strange, Frau Obermann. It is from the Sanskrit. The *sauvastika* or *svastika*. It is frequent in Buddhist manuscripts and inscriptions."

"How did it come to Troy?"

"You must ask your husband. It is quite beyond me. But the sign is found everywhere in antiquity. In my opinion it is an image of the sun in motion. The great wheel, Frau Obermann. The fiery wheel." As he spoke his dead eyes moved upwards, showing the milky retinas.

"I have had that image in my mind all the time." Obermann had been addressing Leonid and Kadri Bey, but now turned to Sophia. "Have I told you of it?"

"Of the wheel, Heinrich?"

"No, no. What are you thinking? It was an engraving in one of my schoolbooks. Aeneas is carrying his father, Anchises, on his shoulders away from the flaming ruins of Troy. There is a look of the greatest fear on the father's face, but Aeneas is calm with the fixed serenity of a higher purpose. He is noble even as the city burns around him. Ever since I saw those high towers falling to the ground, with the smoke and flame billowing around them, I dreamed of finding them again. And here my wife has uncovered a building destroyed by fire! She has found one of the great stone houses of the engraving I revered as a child. Is that not fate? And do you know how all things work together? There are the strangest coincidences in life that would not be permitted in even the most outrageous fiction."

That night she questioned her husband about the marks on the vase and the cup. "Lineau tells me that they are some kind of symbol."

"They may simply be marks, Sophia. Not everything has a meaning."

"They are meaningless?"

"They are decoration. A simple pattern. Such patterns are everywhere in nature. They have no higher purpose."

She sat down upon the side of the bed. For a moment she felt very weary. If there was no higher purpose, what then? What of the pattern of their own lives?

"Come to bed now, Sophia. We have much work to do in the morning. We must catch the worm, as the English say."

SIX

The workmen continued their excavation of the house and staircase the following morning. As the weather grew warmer, some of them began to sleep in the trenches—or even crept into the great stone vases, the pithoi, which lay on their sides in a part of the excavations. Obermann had deemed the area to be an ancient storage-room, but now it had become a dormitory.

The vases were of baked clay, dark red in colour, but protected with a lustrous red wash; they were all cracked and damaged by the pressure of the earth and debris once piled upon them, but, at a size of five or six feet, they afforded protection and coolness for the workers who slept in them. Obermann had named these men the genii of the lamps, because they emerged when bidden from their strange beds. And that morning, on his instructions, they set to work on the burned chamber that Sophia had uncovered. Their progress was slow since they had gradually to remove the mounds of rubbish that had accumulated over many centuries—here were pieces of pottery and small items of bronze, each of which had carefully to be noted and preserved by Leonid and Monsieur Lineau. Obermann always insisted that at half past nine they stop for a breakfast of bread and olives and coffee. He considered, correctly, that the workmen would continue their labours with more enthusiasm after a period of eating and resting. So he called, "*Paidos!*" to the men, and the cry was taken up along the file of diggers.

He sat down with Sophia on a monumental stone that had proved too heavy to remove from the place where it had been uncovered; a figure was carved upon its side, but the features were so eroded that it was no longer recognisable. "I have formed a plan, Sophia," he was saying to her. "I will take you to the place where Paris judged between the three goddesses. There is a glade on the western slope of Mount Ida, which can be reached along a track. There grow three willow trees on that spot, alone among the rocks and the tall grasses, and the inhabitants revere them as sacred. They are known as the ladies of the mountain, and I am convinced that they are some lost memory of Athene, Hera and Aphrodite. Look at the sky, Sophia." An eagle was gliding on the wind, its wings outstretched. "Do you see how its plumage is dark, almost black? Homer calls it *percnos,* monarch of birds. And now look. This is extraordinary." The eagle had seen something moving on the ground, and in an instant it swooped downwards in swift motion. It seemed to fall through the air like some great dark agent of destruction. It fluttered above the dust and stone for a moment, before soaring upwards with a long snake in its beak. Obermann called out to the workers around him, "Look! Omen! Omen! *Oionos!*" He stood up and pointed to the eagle. "The god has sent it skimming downwind. It has appeared on the right side. It brings a blessing to us!" He threw his white canvas hat high into the air, and gave a great whoop of delight. Sophia had never seen him so jubilant.

Kadri Bey had noticed her surprise, and came over to her. "It is an omen of great victory, Frau Obermann. The eagle with the snake in its mouth is a sacred sign to the people. If the bird had approached us from the left, it would mark calamity. But from the right it signals triumph."

"I did not know such things were still believed."

"We are in Troy now. The age of omens has not passed. Look at your husband." Obermann was shaking hands with the workmen.

Instead Sophia observed Kadri Bey with renewed interest. He seemed to summon up for her the strange pieties of this region, where goddesses appeared in wooded groves and where eagles carried snakes into the air. His watchful eyes were now once more upon Obermann, who was handing out piastres. "Your husband is too generous to these men," he said. "They will not feel gratitude. They will ask for more."

"He is joyful, Kadri Bey."

"Your husband is a man of great feeling. I have seen him turn from anger to delight in a moment." Yet his expression seemed to say to her—such men are dangerous.

The omen proved auspicious in one respect. Towards the end of that day's excavation, the Turkish workmen found a small room to the north of the burned site. Sophia noticed at once the remains of a human skeleton. "Heinrich!" She had no need to call him since he had come up behind her and was even then rushing over to the bones.

"This is magnificent, Sophia. Do you see how it is placed?" The skeleton was in a sitting position, slightly inclined against a wall. "I see it with its knees together in fear. Yes. In panic. Do you notice the colour of the bones? This person has been overtaken by the fire and burned to death. By the smallness of the skull I deem it to be a woman, but Lineau will confirm it. What a story this tells! This may be one of Andromache's handmaidens or one of the Trojan wives! And here, what else?" In a corner of the room was a silver vase, some seventeen inches in height. "She was protecting her only possession in the world. What are these women doing?"

The Turkish women, employed to take away the debris and earth, had put down their wicker baskets and had begun a general wailing; they were beating their breasts, and raising their faces to the sky.

"It is a lament, Heinrich, for the dead."

"Good. A lament can do no harm, as long as it does not slow our progress."

Yet there was no more work that day. The Turkish diggers refused to touch the skeleton until it had been the object of ritual purification.

Obermann informed Kadri Bey that he was ready to perform his own ritual for the benefit of the workmen. He suggested that spring water be scattered over the bones during a reading of Homer, but the Turkish overseer considered the idea to be preposterous. "Then we will move it," Obermann said, "with our own hands."

"It must be buried, Herr Obermann. Every minute it is exposed is a dishonour."

"What do I care for your notion of honour when such a gift is presented to us? It is the first skeleton we have found!"

"I resent the way you speak to me, Herr Obermann."

"And I resent your hindering of my work, Kadri Bey. Surely you realise that this is a discovery for science?"

"I cannot allow it."

They argued for several minutes, amid the wailing of the women, but only with the intervention of Sophia was a compromise found. She suggested that Lineau should examine the skeleton where it was placed, and that Leonid should make detailed drawings of it; after that process had been completed, the remains could then be buried on the plain.

"You are a healing force, Sophia. You charm us." Obermann was mopping his face, moist from his recent show of anger.

"Your wife could calm the sea," Lineau said.

"Mark well where it is buried," Obermann whispered to her, as Kadri Bey walked away. "We can always dig it up again."

—◦◦◦—

LINEAU WENT DOWN into the trench, assisted by a Turkish workman, and gently ran his hands across the skull. "Brachycephalic," he said. "Decidedly female." He might have been stroking it. "The face is somewhat broad, with low eye-holes and moderated nose."

"Can you see her, Lineau?" Obermann was peering into the trench.

"Oh, yes. The chin is retracted. The forehead is full. The occiput is broadly expanded."

"And was she beautiful?"

"She is beautiful still." Lineau held the skull in his hands very carefully.

"Draw this beauty, Telemachus. Let the world feast its eyes upon her!"

———✧———

TWO DAYS LATER the skeleton, which Obermann had named Eurycleia, was taken for burial from the mound of Hissarlik to the plain. It was laid in a hastily built coffin of cypress wood, open to the sky, and the bones were scattered with woollen ribbons, garlands of flowers and fresh branches from the trees of the neighbourhood. The women chanted a dirge as the cart trundled down the rough track. Sophia and Heinrich Obermann were at the front of the mourners. "It is a strange thing, Heinrich, to bury one so long dead."

"Eurycleia is not dead, Sophia. She was waiting. She is a messenger. I am sure that we will find other bodies. You know that, during the siege, the handmaidens of Andromache concealed her treasures in a wooden box. She may have been one of those maidens."

There was to be a feast in the village of Chiplak that night as part of the funeral rites. They journeyed from the burial site, which Obermann had carefully noted, and upon entering the village the inhabitants rang the tiny bells that were hanging upon the walls of their dwellings as a sign of good luck. The meal itself, of roasted goat and lamb, was eaten outside in a central area in front of a small mosque. It was already growing dark when Obermann stood up in the middle of the area, and asked the villagers to form a circle around him. He placed a large lantern, similar to those that illuminated the market-stalls in Kannakale, upon the ground. He sat, on a wooden stool, in front of it. The villagers squatted on the earth and, as he instructed, congregated in a circle around the lantern. Then, from memory, he began to recite the opening verses of the *Iliad*. They understood none of it, word for word, and yet certain phrases seemed familiar to them. They murmured to each other at the expressions for the wild fig tree and for the loud, resounding sea. They were caught up in the rise and fall of Obermann's voice as he narrated the doom to come upon Troy. At that point when Agamemnon prayed earnestly to the lord Apollo, the night fell suddenly upon the plain, and the Southern Cross shone far above the horizon. Many beetles had gathered in the space where he sat, and as they scurried forward to the unaccustomed light of the lantern, their hind legs inscribed peculiar markings in the dust. When he narrated the grief of Achilles, Obermann's eyes filled with tears.

After he had finished his recital, some of the villagers stood up and sang in his honour; it was the "song of heroes," known everywhere on the plain of the Troad, and he held out his arms crying, "Good boys! Good boys!" to the singers. Sophia could see that he was exalted. Yet she did not feel that she could share his sense of triumph. He was still apart from her, a person to be studied and observed. "You must allow me to embrace my wife," he said in English. "Come, Sophia. They will see how beautiful you are. Another Helen. You see? Helena."

She came into the circle of light reluctantly, but her entry seemed to be the occasion for music. Three of the villagers came forward with violin, viola and double bass, and at once struck up a vigorous local tune; the violin had four strings, the viola three and the double bass only two, but the battered instruments made a powerful and melodious sound.

Obermann swept up Sophia and began to dance with her in the light of the lantern. As they danced, the players adopted the more formal measures of a waltz, and Obermann stepped more ceremoniously.

"I have not danced a waltz since my wedding," he whispered to her. Then he realised what he had said. There had been no waltz after the marriage ceremony in Athens.

"Wedding? What wedding?"

"It is nothing. It is over."

"What wedding, Heinrich?" She was still waltzing with him, circling in the light. "I was very young."

She walked abruptly out of the light. He ran after her, as the villagers took over the celebration and the music changed.

"I was about to tell you, Sophia. I am a widower. It is long past. Long forgotten."

"Who was she?"

"A Russian. I met her when I was working in St. Petersburg. I soon discovered she was a coarse, vindictive woman."

"And children?"

"None whatever."

Leonid came up then, believing that Sophia had suddenly become ill, but Obermann waved him violently away.

"I give you my word."

"What was her name?"

"Elena Lyshkin. I had almost forgotten it."

"And, one day, will you forget mine?"

Sophia was not surprised that he had once been involved with another woman. But she was horrified that he had told her nothing about it before their wedding. No, not horrified. She felt shame for him. She had inadvertently discovered a weakness, where before she had seen only firmness and strength of purpose. So she became angry with him.

"Was it not your duty, Heinrich, to tell me? To tell my parents? In my country a once married man is very different from a bachelor. Oh, is that the reason? You would have been obliged to pay more."

"That has nothing to do with it, Sophia. I feared that it might disturb you."

"But you were willing to disturb me *after* our marriage. Is that it?"

"It is easier, certainly."

"And what else have you still to tell me, Herr Obermann? Was it *you* who poisoned your mother?" She was very fierce. "Are you a child murderer? A wife murderer? Or perhaps this Elena is still alive?"

"Hush, Sophia. Leonid will hear."

"So the famous Obermann is nervous of gossip. I could laugh."
She turned and, under the anxious gaze of her husband, walked over

to Leonid. Then she came back. She did not look at him. "He is taking us back," she said. "I told him I have the migraine."

On their journey through the soft night they said nothing to each other. But as soon as they had returned to their quarters, she faced him. "*Is* she still alive?"

"No. I have told you. I am a widower. And now the next question. No. I repeat. I have no children. No. I have no connection with her family. Does that satisfy you, Sophia?" He gave a great yell, and seized her. He enveloped her in his arms, and began to blow upon her neck. She struggled to free herself but then, a few moments later, she was laughing.

SEVEN

On the following morning Obermann woke Sophia with a kiss. "You will ride with me to the Hellespont today," he said. "I have had a dream in which we swam together in the waters of a great river. It is a sign."

"I cannot swim, Heinrich."

"Then I will swim on your behalf. I will be your champion."

So they breakfasted together, then rode north towards the shore. From this distance, in the early morning, the Hellespont was an iridescent blue; to Sophia it seemed like some serene band of light between the two shrouded lands of Asia and Europe. Obermann leaned forward and whispered to his horse. "I have told him," he said, "to behave properly in the company of my wife. He understands me perfectly. I called him Pegasus as soon as I purchased him from a horse-dealer in Doumbrek. He is proud of his name." He caressed the horse, and whispered to it again. "I have explained to him that Pegasus was born from the mist of the seas, and that fountains sprang up wherever his hooves touched the ground." He pointed towards the Hellespont. "Onward!" he cried. "Onward to the meeting-place of great seas!"

When they came close to the shore he led the way down a little track that approached a promontory. The waters of the Hellespont had become dark, coloured with green and amber. "The coast of Europe is very close," she said.

"It was once the coast of Greece. Of Thrace."

"One day it may return. Not in my lifetime——"

"Do not talk of lifetimes. We are immortal here! We will conquer the land now. I will swim across the Hellespont and proclaim it to be ours!"

"No, Heinrich. You cannot swim so far."

"Never say 'cannot,' Sophia. Lord Byron declared that he was the first to swim from shore to shore, the first since the time of Leander. But he was a liar. Many have performed that feat."

"Please do not attempt it now, Heinrich, I beg you."

"The story of Hero and Leander will inspire me. The two lovers separated by these waters! The beacon upon the sea-girt tower to light his way across the deep! It is tremendous."

"But Leander drowned, did he not? And Hero flung herself from the rocks."

"That is a later addition, Sophia. It was a fable to explain the division of Europe and Asia. Nothing more."

"It was a charming story, Heinrich."

"Two lovers doomed to early death in the waves? I grant you it has beauty. Yet we will make it more beautiful. Sophia and Heinrich will challenge the Hellespont. Two new lovers will conquer the waters."

Sophia noticed that, to her husband, the comparison did not seem at all fanciful. Now he walked to the shore and, facing the waves, spoke in a loud voice.

"That tale is old, but love anew
May nerve young hearts to prove as true.

"I do not like 'nerve' there," he said. "It is the wrong verb." He came back and stood beside her. "We are the young hearts, Sophia."

"I am not so young any more. And neither are you." The sound of the water was gentle in the early morning.

"Nonsense. We are all young when we come to this place. This is the gateway of the world." He shielded his eyes from the brightness, and looked north. "The Greeks believed that this was the passage into the unknown lands. They gazed northward into the land of the Hyperboreans, who enjoyed an eternal spring. Those people were so near to the stars that they could hear their distant harmonies. They could number the hills upon the moon."

Sophia went down to the edge of the shore, where the water seemed cool and enticing. "What is that island?" she asked him. She pointed to a small patch of land rising above the surface.

"It has no name."

"Why do you not swim there? I cannot bear to see you go further, Heinrich."

"Very well. So be it." He stripped off his shirt and trousers, revealing a bathing suit of somewhat ancient design.

She laughed out loud. "It is what my father wears!" she said. Her father had taken up the new fashion of sea-bathing when he was a young man, and prided himself on the fact that he was still slim enough to wear the same costume.

"Your father is fit. So am I." He walked into the water, calling out to Poseidon as he did so, then launched himself upon the waves with a shout. The water splashed around him as he made his way in the direction of the island: Sophia had never seen anyone make such a commotion. A fishing boat was bobbing on the water nearby; the men were mending their nets, but Sophia could see them laughing and pointing to Obermann. He resembled some small sea-monster, snorting and gurgling in the deep. Within a few minutes he had reached the patch of rock. He hauled himself upon it and began jumping up and down, waving and shouting to her, like a child, eager and excited.

Then he plunged back into the sea, and swam in the direction of the shore. Two or three minutes later she saw him waving again, from the water, but there was something odd—and frantic—about the movement. Then he disappeared beneath the surface. He was in some kind of difficulty. He came up again, but he was not swimming.

He was shouting something to her, but in the prevailing wind she could not hear it. In turn she began shouting and waving to the fishermen still mending their nets. She called in Turkish, *"Imdat! Imdat!"* and pointed at Obermann. One of the men was alerted by her calls for help, and signalled to the others towards the swimmer. Quickly they took their oars and made their way in his direction. To Sophia they seemed to make slow progress, as Obermann went under the waves once more. Then she saw them drag Obermann on board.

She ran down to the shore as the boat made its way back. He was lying in the bottom, upon his side, with his hands clenched into fists. She realised then that he was alive.

They took him from the boat and carried him up the shore, then lowered him carefully on to the dry land of sand and pebbles. She knew only one word of thanks in their language—*"tesekkurler"*—but she repeated it over and over again. She knelt down beside him, but then one of the fishermen grabbed him by the waist, hauled him to his feet, and bent him over. Obermann vomited water for a few seconds, then looked around wearily. "On the ground," he said.

They laid him down, and he seemed to sleep. But then he opened his eyes again, and sprang up as readily and as quickly as if he had been galvanised. She was astonished by his sudden revival. "I had a cramp," he said. "I could not move my leg."

"You were fortunate that these gentlemen were close to you, Heinrich. You must thank them."

He seemed to notice them for the first time. "Thank you, thank you," he said to them in Turkish. "You have saved Heinrich Obermann! The gods will bless you a thousand times! Wait. I will give you something."

He went over to his jacket, lying with his other clothes where he had deposited them before his swim, and took out his wallet. He gave them notes. "Thank you, thank you! You are the sons of Poseidon. You are the warriors of the sea!"

They took the money gladly and, after embracing him, they returned to their boat. "The Greeks would not have taken the money," he said. "They consider life to be the gift of the gods."

"They are poor people, Heinrich. They have families who also deserve to live."

"You are right, of course. I am not complaining. I am merely stating the fact."

"You are fortunate to be alive."

"I know. It was a miracle." He looked back at the waters of the Hellespont. "If they had not been there, I would have been lost in the deep." It seemed to Sophia that he derived a certain gloomy satisfaction from this. "Athene was watching over me. She saved me from the sea-god, just as she saved the heroes of Greece. I am under her protection!"

"You must dry yourself, Heinrich. You will catch cold in the wind."

They rode back soon after; Obermann had become more subdued. "When did you meet the Russian woman?" Sophia suddenly asked him.

"Many years ago. She was fierce and arrogant. I knew nothing."

"Where did you find her?"

"In a small mining town in the east of the country. I had been speculating in Russian gold. Why these questions, Sophia? It is long gone."

"I am interested in the first Mrs. Obermann."

"You have nothing in common with her but the name."

"She was childless?"

"Have I not said so?" He glanced at her. "But you will not remain childless for long. When we have left this place, we will raise a fat and healthy family!"

For some reason the prospect appalled her. "How did she die?"

"She took her own life. She walked into the river."

"I'm sorry."

"There is nothing whatever to mourn. I was glad that she was dead. I felt such relief that I was drunk for three days. Can you imagine Obermann drunk? Well, I was young then."

Sophia did not wish to question him about the suicide. She did not want to entertain the possibility that Obermann had made this woman unhappy. She did not wish to know why she had chosen to kill herself: as she put it to herself, that was not her business. That was not going to be her concern. The past life of a human being was very different from the past of a city such as Troy: it could not be understood. She could no more imagine Obermann and his first wife, twenty years before, than she could imagine meeting him when he was a young man. His previous life was a mystery and, really, she wanted no part in it. It was enough to deal with him in the present moment. But then another question came, unbidden and almost unpronounced. "And your mother? You told me that your father had poisoned her."

"Did I? That was an exaggeration, I'm afraid. She lay sick, and he insisted on making up his own cordial for her. From the berries of the mountains around us. He believed in all the remedies of nature. She died soon after. But I still venerated my father. It was he who first read Homer to me. I have told you this, I know. But it is still as close to me as if I were listening to his voice in the parlour. Do you know what I am hearing? I hear that Athene has shed sweet nectar and ambrosia into the limbs of Achilles so that he will not feel hunger in the battle!" They rode on, Obermann occasionally whispering into the ear of Pegasus. "There is the pillar of Nestor." He pointed to an outcrop of stone that was used as a boundary mark for adjacent fields. "We will soon be home."

EIGHT

We are expecting a visitor, Sophia," Obermann informed her one morning, some days after their ride to the Hellespont. "He has sent me a telegraph from Constantinople to warn me that he is arriving next week."

"Why did you not tell me before? How can I welcome a guest, Heinrich? Look at me." She had adopted the blouse of the Turkish male worker which suited her perfectly. Her hair was tied in a bun, but it betrayed streaks of dust from her recent work in the excavations. Her long skirt was tucked into calico socks, and she was wearing rough leather gloves in order to protect her hands from the stony soil. She insisted that her clothes be washed every evening in the stream a few hundred yards from the mound, but the dust and the mud of each day's digging clung to her. "I am a perfect monster, Heinrich. I cannot be seen."

"Nonsense, Sophia. You are a goddess clothed in the shape of a mortal."

"A dirty mortal."

"This is not dirt. This is the stuff of the ancient city."

"Who is this visitor? We have much work to do, Heinrich."

THEY HAD FOUND the unmistakeable outline of a large chamber that Obermann immediately called "Priam's Throne Room." Many artefacts had been uncovered in the debris that filled the site, among them rings and knives, goblets and pitchers, as well as fragments of figures and shards of pottery. "Do you know what we are missing?" Obermann asked his wife, after a day's labour. "There is one thing we have not yet found. There are no swords."

"That is chance, Heinrich. There will be weapons here."

"Perhaps so. But it is remarkable, is it not, that not one sword has yet been found?"

"And no shields."

He looked at her in astonishment. "You are quite correct. No shields. No swords and no shields. What does that suggest to you, Sophia?"

"I would not like to—"

"I will tell you what it means. If we find nothing of that kind then, as the English say, we are in a pickle. If there are no weapons, then we cannot assume that they were a warlike people. Now do you see?"

"If they were not warlike, then no war," she said. Obermann put his hands up to his ears. "If there was no war," she continued, "then Homer was mistaken."

Obermann had, of course, heard her. "That is a good way of putting it. That is very delicate. Yes." Obermann took off his wide-brimmed hat, and gazed at the sky. "Homer made a mistake. Homer nodded. Do you know that expression, Sophia?" Suddenly he uttered a single, piercing yell that frightened the birds upon the plain beneath. She looked at him in astonishment. "Forgive me, my dear. I am just contemplating the end of my life. If Homer is wrong, then I am wrong." He stamped his foot upon the earth. "This is wrong. Troy is wrong. Everything is wrong. Everything is desolate and gone."

The more perturbed and excited he became, the steadier she held herself. She was very calm. "You are too passionate, Heinrich. Consider. You have found an ancient city where Homer has described Troy. You have found walls. You have found jewellery. What more is needed?"

"Weapons."

"They may have been taken by the Greeks as booty. That is possible, is it not?"

"Possible."

"Or perhaps the Trojans were defeated because they were defenceless."

"In Homer they fought upon the plain and by the river. Hector and Achilles were in combat."

"That is poetry, Heinrich."

"I have lived that poetry. I have believed that poetry. When I was a boy in Furstenberg I was employed in a little grocer's shop. Selling herrings and potato-whisky. That kind of thing. I shall never forget the evening when a drunken man came into the shop. His name was Herman Niederhoffer. He was the son of a Protestant clergyman in Roebel, but had grown unhappy with his lot. So he had taken to drink. Yet he had not forgotten his Homer. He recited to me about a hundred lines of the poet, with all their grand cadence. I asked him to recite them over three times, and each time I gave him a glass of whisky."

"You told me that your father recited Homer to you."

"And so he did. We are German, Sophia. We love the epics. They are part of our life."

Later that day, Obermann took his horse. "I am going to Constantinople," he told his wife. "I must seek wisdom from Ahmed Nedin."

———◦∿∿◦———

"TELL ME about Ahmed Nedin." Sophia turned to Leonid, a few minutes after they had waved farewell to Obermann and watched Pegasus gallop over the plain.

"He is the curator of antiquities at the museum."

"Our treasures here will find their way to him?"

"That is his wish, Frau Obermann. But you must ask your husband."

It was with a certain foreboding, therefore, that she watched him disappear into the distance with a cloud of dust following the trail of his horse.

—⁓—

WITHIN THREE DAYS he had returned. He did not refer to the subject of the weapons, and did not discuss his visit to Constantinople. Instead he seemed more concerned with the imminent arrival of their visitor. "He is a professor at Harvard, Sophia. He has read of my work in the learned journals and has come to pay homage. We cannot turn him away."

"And where will he sleep?"

"There is room in the village."

"Those rooms are filled with bedbugs."

"No matter. In the night, he can think. He can compose articles extolling our virtues."

—⁓—

WILLIAM BRAND had travelled on the packet-boat from Constantinople, where he had been entertained for dinner one night by the American consul. Cyrus Redding had been in charge of the consulate for six years, and professed himself to be what he called a "Turkey fowl," or Turkophile. He loved the wit and vivacity of the people around him. "There is no cleverer race on earth, sir," he said to Professor Brand. "They beat all others."

"They are smart. I give you that."

"More than smart, Professor. They have an old spirit in them. You will see."

"Do you mean the Ottoman?"

"No, sir. Much further back. Considerable further. You are a professor of ancient times, sir, and need no one to tell you."

"Archaeology is not the same as ancient history, Mr. Redding. I wish it was sometimes."

"I mean the Byzantines. And the Greek colonists. The land holds the legacy. Not the bloodline. The land holds everything."

"Not just ruins?"

"Not just ruins." The consul sipped the green tea that a servant had placed before him.

"Hold on a moment. By that reckoning you and I are part Red Indian."

"I don't doubt it for a minute."

The conversation turned to the excavations at Hissarlik. "You must judge whether Obermann has found the fabled city. That's your profession, sir. In my judgement it has been proved. He is a very remarkable man, sir. In some ways he is the most remarkable man of his age. I believe he has acquainted the world with archaeology. He has made it visible."

"Oh, but we are not talking about a circus now," Brand said. "These stunts of his—"

"Stunts? He found the gates and the tombs of Megalopolis. He sailed to Ithaca and found the palace of Odysseus."

"He did not, Mr. Redding. He found some traces of a settlement. Nothing more."

"Did he not? I figured he had. Well, in any case, he came here and by some darned instinct he located the lost city. 'Dig here,' he said. 'It will be here.' That man has genius."

"He is pretty good at showing it, too. Some of my colleagues are considerably displeased with him. He makes them hopping mad. He makes them seem slow."

"He is revered in these parts, Professor. They take pride in their history. They fancy the heroes of Troy to be their neighbours now." He paused and looked steadily at William Brand. "I will tell you something about Obermann, though. Our men of genius may have flaws, may they not?" Brand nodded. "We are both Harvard men, you and I, so I can rely upon your discretion."

"Indeed you can, Mr. Redding."

"Obermann is an American citizen."

"I did not know that." William Brand put his hands behind his head and whistled. "I am mightily astonished, sir."

"You will be more astonished when you learn that he falsified the time he spent in the United States. He bribed four witnesses, to our certain knowledge. He said he had spent five years. He spent four weeks."

"Is that so? I'll be damned."

"Too late now to change it. It would look bad. I'll tell you something else, too. Some months later Herr Obermann was buying up gold dust in Sacramento. He had a contract with a banker in San Francisco. But that contract was torn up. Obermann was sending the banker short weight. Nothing was proven in court since Obermann left before the lawyers got their hands on him. It is mighty interesting, though, is it not?"

"And this doesn't stop him being a great man?"

"Oh, no, sir. It does not. I did not say he was a great man, in any case. I said he was a genius. His flaws make him more interesting."

"They make him more suspect, Mr. Redding."

"That isn't my area. That is yours."

"What do you expect me to do? Spy on him?"

"Nothing of the sort. Goodness me, he is an American citizen."

"By chicanery."

"Never mind. He is a countryman. But I would be mightily interested to know what he is doing down there. The museum people here are exercised about the lack of finds. They don't like it. They believe he may be—how can I put it?—holding back—"

"Keeping the Trojan hoard for himself?"

"That is one way of putting it, Professor. I would not use your exact words."

"So you want me to look around?"

"That is it. Look around. I would like you to keep your eyes open."

NINE

When William Brand stepped off the boat at Kannakale he was greeted by Leonid, who took him at once in the cart to Hissarlik. "You have worked with Herr Obermann for long?" Brand asked him, as they rode over the plain.

"Many years, Professor. I had the honour to be with him in Ithaca. I have seen the house of Ulysses."

"Not many can say that."

"I think of it every day. Prof—" He stopped. Leonid had been advised not to call his employer "professor" in the company of William Brand. "Herr Obermann believes it was there that he slew the suitors of Penelope."

"That is possible, sir, but not probable. I am sure Herr Obermann is aware of the difference."

"Oh, yes! It was one of the first lessons he taught me. *Divide et impera.* Distinguish, and you will be master of your subject."

"Good advice. What is that building over there?"

"Herr Obermann calls it our field hospital. We built it with our own hands from the stones of Troy. Mere rubble. But no finer use could be found for them. We place there all the villagers suffering from malaria. The swamps here emanate dangerous fevers, Professor. Pestilential miasmas. So he thought of this."

"He is a benefactor."

"He reverences the land. And so he reverences the people. Hissarlik is in sight."

William Brand had seen many engravings and photographs of the scene, printed in the American newspapers over the past year. They had depicted the dunes of the ancient river Scamander, the villages on the plain, as well as the mound of Troy itself, with its slopes and ridges and escarpments. Nevertheless, he was surprised by its dignity. That was the only word he could find for the effect it had upon him. He knew that it would be a place of busy, almost incessant, activity; even now, from this distance, he could see the workmen with their carts and pickaxes moving over the earth. He knew also the dirt and discomfort of any excavation. But there was an additional quality here. The curious notion occurred to him that, Troy being found, the earth had breathed a sigh of relief. It had given up its burden.

"You see, Professor, that we are working upon the entire site. Herr Obermann wishes for a complete picture of the city."

"Is that wise, sir? Much depends on the patient examination of one area. There are so many levels that need to be thoroughly examined—"

"We are limited in time. Our permit lasts for only one more year. And then—who knows?—the English or the Swiss may come."

"And steal your baby?"

"It is Herr Obermann's baby. He found it. He adopted it. He gave it a name."

"But then you must consider its true paternity, sir. The government of this region must judge who is allowed to come here."

"Herr Obermannn will argue with you." Leonid laughed. "And he has a wife who will join him. Frau Obermann has opinions of her own."

"I had no notion that he was married."

"Frau Obermann is a Greek woman. Young and beautiful, if I may say so."

"Is she now?"

"But she works with us all. She does not sit in her tent, as Homer would say. She joins in the field work and the excavations. It was Frau Obermann who found the skeleton."

"Skeleton?"

"Already I have said too much. You will meet her soon enough, Professor."

———

IN FACT it was Sophia who greeted William Brand as the horse and cart came up to the mound. "My husband is occupied at the present," she said in English. "I am your guide for an hour or so, Professor Brand. I hope that does not inconvenience you."

"On the contrary, ma'am, it is very convenient. I had not expected so charming a companion."

"But I am not erudite. I am not *au fait* with all the work."

"I hear that you are at the centre of everything."

"From Leonid? He exaggerates. May I bring you some coffee? It is only Turkish, I'm afraid."

After they had finished their coffee, which William Brand found excessively muddy, she led him slowly among the pits and trenches. "We have found six levels," she told him. "Six different settlements over a period of two thousand years. Each time the city was rebuilt on the partial ruins of its predecessor."

"That is decidedly queer."

"Monsieur Lineau—you will meet him later—has a theory about it. He believes that the city had some sacred image, or some sacred space, that had to be preserved. The city was here to protect it."

"I know of no other city like it, if that *is* the case. Except that my colleagues in Mexico have found a strange city of temples that defies explanation. Maybe Troy is related."

"No. It is singular, Professor Brand. It is the original. My husband is very clear about that. It is the first city."

"That's too much speculation for me, ma'am. I like to see the material with my own eyes. I like to feel the stone with my hands."

"Then look around you. You will see everything. In this trench, to your right, you will see signs of calcination. My husband believes that we have uncovered a portion of a tower from the second city. He believes it to be part of the burned and ruined city of Homer. The pottery here is of a lustrous red, unique to this level. But you will soon read that in your newspapers."

"Indeed. At home it is a matter of great excitement and debate. But I would like to see the evidence."

"Polemon, who lived in the second century before Jesus Christ"— she bowed her head at the sacred name—"came to Troy. He remarked that he had seen there the identical altar of Zeus on which Priam had been slain. He had also seen the stone upon which Palamedes taught the Greeks to play at dice. That is evidence of the monuments to be found here, is it not?"

"You are remarkably well informed, Mrs. Obermann."

"I have a good teacher."

"I would say that you are more learned than my graduates."

"Oh, no. Not learned. I have been able to pick up scraps of knowledge very quickly. My husband is continually explaining matters to me. He is helping me all the time." She suddenly ceased to be serious, and laughed at his bemusement. "You do not believe a female can speak of Polemon and ancient Troy. Is that it?"

"Oh, no, ma'am. That is not any cause of astonishment. I am just considering how a pretty young woman can be so in love with mud and stone. Forgive me. Yankee plain speaking."

"I am not in the least offended." She laughed again. "I surprise myself sometimes, Professor Brand. Let me show you the outer wall." She led him to an outcrop of stones that had been fashioned to fit one another without mortar, "In the legend, of course, this wall was built by Poseidon and Apollo."

"Or by Poseidon alone."

"You recall the passage? 'I built a wall broad and fair, so that the city might not be taken.'"

"You have a fine memory, Mrs. Obermann."

"I study that book. I almost have it by heart now. My husband reads it to us every evening, and then I go back to the words themselves. To the original Greek."

William Brand was already half in love with Sophia Obermann, although he would not have admitted this to himself; he led a bachelor existence in Harvard University, where he lived in a white wooden-framed house in a street off the Green. He was a tall, lean man, redolent of the New England family from which he came; he had the slight stiffness, the exaggerated politeness, of his stock. He exhibited what Bostonians regarded as "rectitude," an uprightness of manner and straightness of dealing. He was not effusive. He did not have what he called "the New York bounce," by which he meant a certain snappiness and glibness. He had never married because, as he told his friends, he did not know how to "go about" a courtship or proposal; he was, in effect, too shy. On any topic concerned with his subject, however, he was precise and even on occasions argumentative. His politeness, in his profession, was limited. In private he cursed the strictness of his upbringing, yet on Sundays he still always worshipped at the Unitarian chapel.

Now with Sophia Obermann, on the windy mound of Troy, he found that he could speak freely. "I read Homer as a child," he said, "in Longfellow's translation. Our American poets have a fine line in exuberance, but I think Mr. Longfellow was thinking of Red Indians rather than of Trojans."

"Did you never study Greek?"

"Oh, yes. It was drilled into us at Deermount—that was my school—until we ate and drank Greek. Yes, ma'am, we knew our Greek. I remember our master saying that the Greek victory against the Persians was more important in human history than the American defeat of the British. That shook us up a bit. But we never doubted it."

"I have studied the history of my people, too. But only now—"

"Is it coming alive for you?"

"That is the phrase. Coming alive. This is what I wanted to show you. You see these lines just inside the wall?" She showed him a rectangular section of stone, barely emerging out of the earth. "It is a different material from the wall. It is of marble. I believe it to be an altar built against the wall as a holy defence."

"There were such altars, ma'am. I give you that."

"And I believe I know what altar it is. It is the altar of Ate mentioned by Lycophron and by Apollodorus. She is strong and swift. She walks with light, soft feet over the heads of men. We know that she was worshipped on this hill by the Trojans, and what better place for the goddess of strength than the wall itself?"

"It is a theory. If I put you in front of a class of Harvard men, they would believe you in a minute. You have considerable conviction, if I may say so. But it is only a theory."

"I grant you that, Professor. But are theories not sometimes beautiful?"

"Not if they get in the way of facts."

She stamped her foot upon the ground. "But this is the fact." He feared that he might have upset her. "I am not angry. I am merely stating that this earth beneath our feet is a fact. We have too many facts. We have not enough theories."

"Well, ma'am, that is unusual. In my profession it is generally the other way round."

"Ah, here is my husband."

Obermann had come on to the plateau behind them. "I have found it, Sophia!" He hastened over to them. "Forgive me, forgive me, Professor Brand, for not greeting you more formally. I am Obermann." He bowed and shook the American's hand. "Welcome to our little city. I have found it, Sophia! You have come on a day, Professor, that will go down in the annals of archaeology. I have found a Trojan sword! I have found a bronze sword!"

"That is wonderful news, Heinrich." Sophia was looking expectantly, almost curiously, at her husband. "You had almost given up hope of discovering such a thing."

"Never give up hope! Is that not right, Professor? Do you not teach that at Harvard? Never give up hope of finding marvels."

"I would be highly interested in seeing this sword, Mr. Obermann."

"You will be the first among all your colleagues to gaze upon it. Come. We will approach the long-lost wonder."

He led them towards the other side of the hill, looking east. As they walked across the area of excavation, he was very gleeful. He pinched Sophia's arm and blew her a kiss. "Oh, Professor," he said. "Watch where you are walking."

"Pardon me?"

"I mean it literally. Watch. Observe. Do you notice anything about the track?"

"I see limestone."

"Yes. Good. You see flags of limestone, actually. It is an ancient street. But what else do you see?"

"Nothing."

Obermann laughed. "Good. Very good. Nothing. That is precisely what I see. Nothing." He laughed out loud again. "And what do you deduce from that, Professor?"

"Sir?"

"When the dogs do not bark, you must ask for a reason. That is what we were taught in Germany."

"I don't quite follow your line of thought."

"There are no ruts. *Ergo,* no chariot wheels. This street served only for pedestrians."

William Brand whistled. "Now that is something. I take my hat off to you, sir."

"You have no hat. I strongly advise you to get one."

"An American expression. I am mightily impressed."

"It is nothing. Experience. Practice, my dear sir. I will tell you something else about the limestone, Professor. It contains mussel shells."

"I beg your pardon?"

"Mussel shells. In the far reaches of the past, there was a freshwater or brackish lake upon this spot. Now I will show you the sword."

Sophia was surprised at the unexpected and wholly fortuitous discovery of the weapon, but she resolved not to question her husband about the matter. Not in front of the American.

"The sword, dear Professor," Obermann was saying, "is the symbol of Homer. It is the key to this truth."

"Yet the sword is no proof in itself that there was a war between the Greeks and the Trojans."

"You must not leap to conclusions."

William Brand was surprised. "Pardon me, sir, but I am not the one leaping to conclusions. Surely——"

"You mistake me. I am not speaking of truth in your sense. I am speaking of truth in a larger sense. What is the purpose of life?"

"That's a pretty deep subject, sir."

"The purpose of life is to learn how to die. That is the great theme of Homer. That is the meaning of this sword. Here. It is here." They had come up to the hut in which many of the finds were kept. "This is our holy room, Professor. I wished to take you on an extended tour as soon as you arrived, but the gods have decreed otherwise. Come." He led the way towards the long wooden table where the most recently discovered objects were placed. "Is it not a beauty?" A piece of thin bronze was lying upon a cloth, some nine inches long and two inches broad; it was severely decayed, flaking away and mottled with vermilion and verdigris rust. "I have read your paper on the weapons found in Wisconsin, Professor. The axes were of pure copper, were they not?"

William Brand was surprised that he had seen his paper, published recently in a periodical entitled *Early American Archaeology.* "Of copper, yes. I am delighted that you range so far in your reading."

"It is my business to do so. And so the question remains. From where did the Trojans obtain their tin to make bronze? And I have the answer. It came from Cornwall in England. It was carried by Phoenician traders. I was alerted when an unknown goblet was found in a little town called Mevagissey. I do not know what the name means. I have not yet mastered Celtic. I saw a drawing of this goblet in the London *Times,* and I knew it at once. It was Homeric, two-handled. There was a connection between these two places, Professor, which brought in bronze. No one else knows of this as yet. You may wonder why I mentioned your battleaxes in Wisconsin." William Brand was bewildered by Obermann's restless, impatient, emphatic manner of speaking. "We found the remains of a battleaxe beside this sword. It was so much destroyed by chloride of copper that it fell into minute fragments even as I took it out."

"Why did you make such haste to remove it?"

"It was dissolving into the earth—"

"No. Not the battleaxe. The sword. It is in a very delicate condition, and cannot last in the air. Why take it out?"

"I have been waiting to find this all my life, Professor Brand. And you ask me why I bore it in triumph to this place of safety? It is not a question to put to one such as I."

"You could have destroyed the evidence you are looking for. It is not wise."

"Wise? I am not wise. I am a fanatic. I am a fanatic for knowledge. *Episteme.* You understand me, of course, Sophia." She had been standing in the doorway, not wishing to come any nearer. "Scientific understanding."

"I must just say, sir, that there is nothing scientific about it. That has struck me in the short time I have been here. You have built a trench like the Grand Canyon through the mound, and expect to find a great city waiting for you."

Obermann seemed genuinely puzzled by Brand's criticism. "I beg your pardon, Professor. I bow to your superior experience. Of the Grand Canyon, I mean."

Sophia now came forward. "No doubt Professor Brand would like to examine Priam's palace, Heinrich."

"And that's another thing," Brand said. "We do not know if anyone by the name of Priam ever lived here."

Obermann tapped Sophia on her cheek. "Do you see how you have upset the professor?" Then he turned to Brand. "I will defend my wife, Professor, until Troy sinks below the earth. And let me tell you something. I shall allow her to call him by the name of Priam until you prove to me that he had another name. Would you care for our Turkish coffee?"

IN THE EARLY EVENING Brand expressed a desire to examine the finds more carefully.

"As you wish," Obermann replied. He took off his hat, and wiped the inside with his handkerchief. "But I must insist that you take no notes. Much remains to be published."

Brand was dismayed by Obermann's apparent lack of trust. "Surely you do not think that I would anticipate—"

"I have learned that this is a hard business, Professor. Worldly reputation is meaningless to me, but I cannot allow my work to be divulged before its time."

"I had no thought of that, sir."

"Good. Come. This is our museum." There was an annexe to the main hut, where many objects were stored in wooden trays or boxes placed upon a makeshift set of shelves. Brand began to examine the handwritten slips pasted upon each of them, detailing the location and the level at which they had been found. Then he took down one of the boxes.

"This cannot be right, Mr. Obermann."

"I beg your pardon?" Obermann had been standing behind him, watching him keenly and impatiently.

"You have two different types of pottery in this box, but they are marked to have come from the same level. This is a tripod basin of terracotta, and this is a simple vase-cover. They are centuries apart, sir."

"The pottery was the same at Troy Two as at Troy Five. What of it?"

"It is not possible."

"Do not tell me what is possible, Professor. If I had heeded that, I would have achieved nothing."

"I am a blunt man, sir. Excuse me for speaking out of turn, but it just makes no sense."

Obermann frowned, and looked at the box of finds. "Now all is clear to me. The basin must have washed down from a higher stratum. I remember that it rained all night before we reached this level. That is the simple truth of the matter."

"Then surely you should distinguish them?"

"There is no time."

"You must distinguish them."

" 'Must' is not a word for Obermann." He looked very fierce, but then he relented. "Let them perform the work in Constantinople. It will give them something to do."

TEN

On the following day Leonid brought William Brand from his lodging in the nearby village, where he had just breakfasted on bean paste and black tea. Brand had not spent a comfortable night. He had been given a Turkish straw mattress, laid upon the ground, and had soon discovered that it contained vermin or what he remembered from the Bible as "crawling things." So he spent the rest of the night sitting against a wall, legs against his chest, with a blanket around his shoulders. He vowed not to go back. He would rather sleep in the trenches of Hissarlik. His mood improved, however, as they drove in the early morning towards the mound. There were some white stones and columns to the east, which he had not seen during the evening ride into the village. "That looks to me," he said out loud, "like a temple."

Leonid glanced in the same direction. "It is called Hagios Demetrios Tepeh. It is by a hill dedicated to St. Demetrios. You are quite right, Professor. The columns are the remains of a Greek temple."

"This place is a wonder. It is like some living piece of the ancient world. Has the temple been examined?"

"We do not have the men to spare. Besides, they will not go there."

"Why ever not?"

"It is well known for fever. It is supposed to be cursed."

"They hold on to their old superstitions, do they?"

Leonid looked at him in surprise. "Of course. You tread on sacred ground, Professor. Do you see that hill there? Due east? With the trees growing in front of it? That is one of the fearsome places. There is a cave there, which if you enter, the locals say, you will lose your shadow."

"I sure would like to visit that place."

"Oh, you cannot. Herr Obermann forbids it."

"Forbids it?"

"He may not have faith in the religion, but he has faith in the people. He would not oppose their beliefs in any way."

"That is a rum way to manage an enterprise, sir."

"We are in their world, Professor. We must obey its laws."

"I am a free citizen, sir. I do not boast of it, but it is a fact. Would Mr. Obermann prevent me travelling where I wish?"

"You must ask him."

"I sure am interested in that cave."

William Brand had been raised by his Unitarian parents to respect what was known as the "rational religion." The age of miracles had passed, as they taught him, and they had impressed upon him the values of public service, good works, thrift and success. He argued with his friends that it was not necessarily an arid faith, since it had taught him modesty and a sense of honour, but he agreed that it was not an exciting one: it possessed little of the sublime and the mysterious that, instead, he pursued through his explorations of lost cultures. He had an appetite for the remote past, for the masterworks of ancient civilisations fallen into ruin, for cryptic symbols on old stone.

"What is the cave called?" he asked Leonid. "Does it have a name?"

"It is known as the cave of Semele."

"She was the mother of Bacchus, was she not?"

"An unfortunate lady, Professor. When her lover, Jupiter, came down in all his glory, she burned to death in his brightness."

"But surely she is not from this region? She came from Thebes."

"Her sorrowful son brought her ashes here. Or so it is said. They lie within the cave. It is called *lagoum* by the villagers."

The cave had been well known for many generations, and had never lost its reputation as a fearful place. On one day of the year the local villagers formed a procession, and led a cow to its entrance. The animal was slaughtered there, and left for the ghosts or demons. The carcass was always gone by the following morning, and the villagers swore that it had not become the prey of wolves or wild dogs. It had been eaten by the dwellers of the *lagoum*. It was also said that, if you entered the cave and somehow managed to evade those who dwelled within it, you would come out on the other side of the world in a place where the sea was above you and the sky beneath your feet.

———

OBERMANN GREETED BRAND when they drew up to the mound. "Did you sleep well, Professor? The air here is very restful."

"I was not alone, Mr. Obermann. I had uninvited guests."

"I beg your pardon?"

"Vermin. Bedbugs, we call them."

"We call them that also." Obermann laughed, and took Brand's arm. "No matter. We are far above them now. Our present height above the sea is one hundred and nine feet. Our height above the plain is fifty-nine feet. Yet it would once have been lower. Follow me across this gap. I calculate that with the alluvia of the river the land has risen twenty feet in two thousand years. Am I right in that calculation, Professor?" Brand was still catching his breath, having leaped across a trench and jumped from one great stone to another. "You must swim in the Hellespont. Your lungs will be magnified. The ancient historians claim that Troy had not been entirely destroyed, but that it always remained inhabited and never ceased to exist. I agree with them. Human beings are creatures of habit and of instinct. They dig in old mounds. They search out old corners. Is that not so? Why do dogs love the smell of urine?"

"I have no notion."

"It is a primitive smell. It was the same smell when these stones lived."

Brand had stopped, in order to survey the scene of the workings. "In your latest report to *The Times,* Mr. Obermann, you mentioned a tower."

"Of course. It is there. Do you not see it rising out of the earth?"

"I see a piece of a wall. Nothing more."

"Look again, Professor. It is the tower that Andromache ascended because she had heard that the Trojans were hard pressed and that the power of the Achaeans was great."

"I know the passage, Mr. Obermann. But I'll be darned if I can see the tower."

"No matter. We have a different vision." He led Brand forward quickly. "Near the surface of the ruins here I found a large house belonging to a great man, because the floors were made of large slabs of red stone excellently polished."

"A high priest, perhaps?"

"You are using your imagination, Professor. I congratulate you. Yes. A high priest. One who ascended the tower, which you refuse to see, and greeted the sunrise and rosy-fingered dawn. But I dug deeper. I was interested in what lay beneath. And what did I find? Immense masses of burned and partly vitrified bricks! Ancient Troy! Mr. Gladstone has told me, in a personal letter, that I deserve the gratitude of the entire civilised world. I am inclined to believe him."

"You call it Troy Two in your report, sir. But surely from the pottery it is a thousand years too early to be the Troy of Homer. All the objects I have seen are from the early Iron Age."

"And the bronze sword?"

"That just complicates matters. I was considering the problem last night. It cannot come from that level."

"The bedbugs have got into your head, Professor. Tell me, in Harvard, do you not still use the furniture of your grandmother?"

Brand had indeed inherited an oaken settle and a dining-table from his grandparents. "I do."

"So there are two periods in your house, are there not? They are, so to speak, both at the same level."

"But a thousand years—"

"In this region a thousand years is nothing. Change is slow. Habits are enduring." Brand did not reply. "My judgements are based on evidence, dear sir. If you could have seen what mounds of earth had to be removed, to get a view of the lower levels, you would scarcely believe that a single man in the course of one year could have accomplished so great an undertaking. I have extracted the nucleus of the hill, Professor Brand."

"Around the nucleus revolve many separate parts, Mr. Obermann. I am worried that they have fallen away."

"Do not worry. Worry is not wise. It taxes the strength."

"We Yankees are great worriers. It is in the blood."

"Ah. Is that so? It would explain the hysterics concerning Mamashkaui Bay." He was referring to a controversy of the year before, when at an inlet by the New England shore the remains of an ancient settlement had been found. It had been dated to the late tenth century A.D. and was naturally considered to be that of the native Indians. But, in the following weeks, there had been discovered a stone lamp, a ship repair piece made of wood, a soapstone spindle whorl and a copper alloy ring head pin. The last two were of characteristically Norse design, and the materials were the same as those found at sites in Iceland and in Greenland. The "hysterics" to which Obermann referred came from North American historians who refused to believe that Norsemen or Vikings had landed—and inhabited—America many centuries before its official discovery by Christopher Columbus. "You will find other settlements," Obermann was saying. "I am sure of it. Have your colleagues not read the Norse sagas?"

"They are being studied now, I believe. Everything has been thrown into doubt."

"You will read there of voyages to a fabled land called Vinland, filled with grapes and wheat. There were battles between the Vikings and the natives of that place who were called *skraelings.*"

"I know of this." Brand had held long conversations into the night with a colleague in the Faculty of History, Professor Albright, who was alternately shocked, dismayed and excited by this new perspective on the American past.

"You must learn to trust the sagas, Professor. Is that not the lesson I have taught you all? If I go to America, I am sure to find a Viking longboat!" He looked out towards the Hellespont. "Tell your colleagues to dig a little eastward from the settlement. They will find a burial place with several dead."

Brand was puzzled. "I am not sure how——"

"The word 'mamashkaui' in the native Indian tongue means 'the killing disease.' They applied it to the smallpox brought over by the foreigners. That is why it is named Mamashkaui Bay."

"I am astonished, sir."

"These Norsemen lived and died in America, Professor. They were destroyed by illness, not by the natives. The last ones would have buried their companions to the east, in the path of the rising sun." Even as he spoke, in an area of land a few hundred yards east of Mamashkaui Bay, the archaeological team were finding signs of inhumation burials. "But Obermann will speak only of Troy. Do you see the mass of earth partly slid down the slope, Professor? This is where we threw our debris. So from a distance the hill seems to be growing continually larger and larger. It now looks more stately than ever it did before. And this is the curious thing. It resembles a fortress more obviously than at any other time in its history. It is perfecting its nature. It is becoming what it was once described as being. But that will be too poetical for you, Professor. Excuse me. It smacks of German romance."

"Not at all, Mr. Obermann. I have a deal of poetry in myself, if I may say so. But one thing does puzzle me."

"Yes?"

"In your report in *The Times* you say that the palace was built on the summit. But it is here, on the north-west ridge."

"It is necessary to inspire the readers of your newspapers. To give them dreams. That is my idealism, Professor. In my imagination I witnessed the gleaming palace surmounting all. It will be rectified in the book. Do you see here the sculpted splinters of white marble? A temple. Too late for our purposes."

William Brand was surprised by his nonchalance. He had never met anyone like Obermann before, and he did not know how to proceed with him. Yet he felt emboldened by him. It was like entering some new territory, where previous laws and customs need not apply. "I was considering last night, sir, that you had told another tall story."

"A *tall* story?"

"An invention. A fantasy."

"You credit me with too much ingenuity, Professor."

"You stated in *The Times* that you had found a statuette and rings concealed in a wall of the palace. You suggested that they were hidden as the invaders stormed the building."

"What of it?"

"From my memory I believe that those objects were found at different levels. So it said upon the labels. They could not have been concealed at the same time."

"The story is more important, Professor. Stories brought me to this place. What would happen if the world were without stories?"

"But you have combined two finds. Your story is untrue."

"What is truth?"

"I can't answer that. But I do know what is false."

"You are being ridiculous. My story, as you call it, has fixed an essential element in Troy. The finds themselves are of no interest to me in isolation."

"That is where we differ."

"And where we will continue to differ. I am here to re-create Troy, not to reduce it to a pile of dust and bones. Now, if you will excuse me, I must organise the day's digging."

He walked off, his cane hammering upon the ground, and Sophia watched him adjust his pocket-watch with more than usual intentness. She came over to him. "Our American friend," he said, "is nervous and dyspeptic. Like some hysterical female. He vexes himself over trifling matters. Newspaper articles! Bedbugs!"

"You are becoming angry, Heinrich." She looked at her husband with an almost impersonal interest.

"He has no feeling for this place."

"Oh, you may be wrong. Leonid tells me that Professor Brand wishes to visit the cave of Semele."

"Oh? Does he?" He looked around at William Brand. "Has he been made aware of its history?"

"Leonid has told him the story."

"And it does not make him fearful?"

"It does not move him in the least."

"Is that so?" Obermann smiled. "Then we must arrange a horse for him. No one will take him."

"Is it wise for him to go alone, Heinrich?"

"Professor Brand is a rational man. He does not fear. Where there is no fear, there is nothing to be feared."

"I would like to go with him."

"No! I utterly forbid it! *Absolument pas!*" She was surprised by his fierceness. "I speak out of love and devotion for you, Sophia. You are a child of Greece. You may not know of it, but you are filled with superstition. The American has nothing to lose. Nothing to gain, but nothing to lose."

She would be dutiful in this, of course. Her mother had taught her that a wife obeys her husband in small requests so that she might rule him in more important matters. Yet Sophia thought that she had discovered a better way. She had learned that if she embraced her duties with enthusiasm those duties ceased to be burdensome. That is why she had immersed herself in Homer, and why she took pride in her excavations. She had become Frau Obermann rather than Sophia Chrysanthis. Was that not what it meant to be married?

"Yet I can guide him there, can I not, Heinrich? That can do no harm."

"Stay far away from the cave, Sophia. The people do not treat it with abhorrence for no reason."

ELEVEN

S ophia accompanied Brand eastward across the plain. "This is all table-land," she said. "Where the horses are reared."

"The Trojans were famous horse-trainers, were they not?"

"Oh, yes. And they used exactly the same land for it. We have found nothing on this ground. Not even bricks or fragments of pottery. Everywhere the natural soil, as it was then and as it is now."

"You have a musical tone to your voice, Frau Obermann. Like a singer."

"Have I?"

"No one has told you before?"

"It has never been mentioned, Professor." She laughed. "I certainly cannot sing."

"I believe that you are not used to compliments."

"I do not deserve them."

"Oh, you do. You deserve every compliment in the world."

"Now you flatter me."

"As we say in America, you would be nice to come home to." She remained silent. "Forgive me. I have gone too far."

"Do you see ahead of you the ridge of hills?"

"There is the cave, is it not?"

"Nothing grows there. It is said that the branches of trees turned towards this place wither away."

"That's mighty interesting."

"It *is* interesting, Professor. I wish that I could come with you, but my husband—"

"Your husband is too swayed by stories, Mrs. Obermann. Do you believe in ghosts and suchlike?"

"I do not believe in them." She spoke very slowly, and then hesitated. She looked towards the mouth of the cave as they approached it. "But I think I am afraid of them. I must stop here, Professor. I will wait for you."

———

HE RODE FORWARD, more quickly without his companion, and came up to the cave. His horse reared as they approached the entrance, startled perhaps by a snake, but he whispered to it and patted it down. He tethered the animal to an outcrop of stone, and walked forward.

He stopped at the threshold, and lit a lantern that he had brought with him. Then he entered the mouth of the cave. It was not as cool as he had expected, inside the cave, but there was a passage of air coming from within. The floor was a smooth surface, with a few stones or pebbles scattered in the grey dust. There were some overhanging rocks that appeared to be of the same colour and texture as the dust, but petrified and twisted into strange shapes. There was no odour of damp or decay but of something mild and fusty; he was reminded of the time he had opened the wardrobe in his father's bedroom, and smelled the frock-coats and overcoats hanging within. And there was no noise; the dust at the entrance to the cave was so thick and so fine that his steps were muffled. The rock had also closed off any sound from outside; he could no longer hear his horse pawing upon the ground. He held up the lantern, but its light did not seem to penetrate very far into the cave; there was a pearly iridescence in front of him, and then no more. He could still sense the passage of air coming from some gap or vent, but it seemed in his heightened state to have become warmer. Or was that simply the still, dry air within the cave? He called "Hello!" There was no echo. He turned to look back but the bright light of the lantern must have concealed the entrance, and the daylight, from him. He took a long stride but then he stumbled; he fell forward before righting himself with a sudden instinctive movement. The lantern swung wildly in his hand, and for a moment it seemed as if his shadow had passed him, stopped and looked back.

———❧———

SOPHIA HAD BEEN WAITING for half an hour or so. A sea-wind, carrying dampness from the Aegean, passed over the plain and refreshed her. It presaged travels and partings, but she welcomed it. Then Professor Brand came out of the cave. He was standing upright, and walking very slowly. He walked past his horse, which looked curiously at him but made no sign of movement. Brand's head was held at an angle, as if he had injured his neck, and as he came closer she could see that he was staring straight ahead. Something was wrong. His skin had taken on a grey colour.

"I must go home," he said, when he came up to her. He was not looking at her.

"You have caught a chill in the cave, Professor. This is not healthy ground."

"Home."

She went over to his tethered horse and took one swift glance into the interior of the cave. It seemed very light, and she guessed that the rays of the sun had found a crevice somewhere within the rock. She led the horse away. Professor Brand was still standing, his head twisted awry, and with some effort she managed to haul him on to the horse where he sat bowed upon the leather saddle. Then she mounted her own horse and, holding the reins of Brand's animal with one hand and guiding hers with the other, she made her way back to the village where Brand had slept the previous night. By good fortune Leonid was there, buying some sacks of wheat, and she called out to him.

He came hurrying over.

"He must have caught some sickness in the cave," she said. "Some fever."

They took him from the horse and half dragged, half carried him into the peasants' house. Three women were sitting in the secluded garden, grinding a heap of sesame seeds, and Leonid explained that the professor had returned to his bed because of sickness. He did not mention the *lagoum* of Semele. The women got up at once, fearful of the fever that often spread through the region. But when they saw the American being helped to the pallet bed by Sophia, they noticed at once that there was no heat or sweat coming from him. He was pale, his lips and eyes grey. They turned away, and left the house without looking back.

The men did not return to the house after that day's labour, but stayed with their cousins at the other end of the village.

———∽∽———

SOPHIA REMAINED by the bedside all that afternoon and evening. Brand lay upon the straw mattress, breathing slowly and heavily. His eyes were open, but he made no sign. It was as if he were lost in thought. But then, just as the sun was setting, he turned his face towards Sophia and seemed to look at her. "Dancers," he said.

Obermann, alerted by Leonid, arrived a few minutes later. He went over to the bed and glanced down at Brand. "There is no strength in him," he said. "He is a shadow. Did you heed my warning, Sophia?"

"I did not enter."

"Do you see what may happen when we thwart the will of the gods?" He bent over and felt Brand's pulse. "I cannot give him quinine. This is not a fever. And there is no need for laudanum. He is not in pain. Do you see how his face has lost its lines? He is going back."

"To America?"

"No, no, Sophia. That is too short a journey. He is going back to his origins." Then he knelt down and inspected the straw mattress. "It is as I expected," he said. "Even the bedbugs have fled." He went outside and stood next to Leonid, looking out at the darkening plain. "We cannot deal with these matters, Telemachus. They are above us."

"Will he recover?"

"Of course not. You must telegraph the American consul. He must be taken back to Constantinople. We cannot have his body here. It will curse our work. The villagers are already in a state of fear. I have promised them money, but he cannot stay here for very long." Obermann went back into the house. "You sit here, Sophia, like a goddess on a funerary monument. As lovely as marble!"

"Heinrich!"

"Excuse me. My apologies. I cannot speak of beauty in these circumstances." He went over to Brand, and looked down at him again. Brand's eyes were still open, and he seemed to be breathing normally. "He is waiting. Are you happy to stay with him until the morning?"

"Naturally."

"You *are* a goddess."

"If I were, I could help him."

"You have no thought of yourself in this situation, Sophia. I admire that. It is as it should be. I can assure you that you are in no danger. This is not an infection."

"Then what is it?"

"It is a sickness. But it is not a sickness of the body. I know no more than that. You must ask a priest of the Turks."

"The only word he said to me was 'dancers.' "

"Dancers? The plain is known as the dancing plain, when the wheat is tossed and lifted by the wind."

"Could he have meant that?"

"And there were dancers who accompanied the gods when they visited mortals. But who can fathom the mind in such a condition?"

———ᨆ———

SHE STAYED with William Brand all that evening and night. She began to enjoy the silence, of which there had been so little in these first months of marriage. She settled back within it, looking at Brand from time to time and even taking his hand. He seemed to her to be sleeping, despite the fact that his eyes were still open. If this is death, she thought, then I need not fear it. Yet who knew? She had heard of spells that were cast upon people for days or weeks, before they were lifted. She had heard stories of people waking after they had been presumed dead. Then once again she allowed the silence to enter her for an hour or more.

"I do not love him," she said at last. "But I admire him." She was silent again. "He is not an ordinary man." Again there was silence. "You were quite right to question him. He needs to be questioned. He will run off in all directions if he is not corrected. His excitement and enthusiasm lead him to do odd things. If you had asked him about the sword, I do not know what answer he would have given you. It is a puzzle. I do not wish to think of it. The husband of Frau Obermann must be above suspicion!" She laughed. "You ask me why I married him. I had no choice in the matter. My mother had decided for me. But that is not such a bad thing. It removes all doubts and uncertainties. I can go on with my life without years of waiting. I say 'my life.' But is it my life? I did not think it would be this." She stopped and placed Brand's right arm beneath the blanket. It felt curiously light. "When I first came to this place, I was dismayed. What had I to do with Troy? But then Monsieur Lineau told me of the gods—oh. Forgive me." She looked at Brand's face, which remained calm and immobile. "There is salvation in work. In activity. As soon as I began to dig I found a purpose. It is what my husband calls my destiny. I do not think it is that precisely. It does not seem like my destiny. I will know it, when it comes. But this is not it." She sighed, and went over to the door; she tried to glimpse, through the night, the outlines of the wild olives growing out of the rocky ground below. She saw nothing but darkness. "I have told him that I do not want children as yet. It is not what a Greek wife is meant to say. Yet he has accepted it. He is very like a child himself, don't you think? He does not need a rival. Imagine my astonishment when my husband came into our bedroom the other night, knelt before me, put his head into my lap and burst into tears! It was entirely unexpected. Then he left." She came away from the window, and resumed her seat beside the bed. "I do not think that I will ever have children. That is my opinion. He is older than me, of course. Much older. But it makes no difference to me. He has been married before. I did not know that until I came here." She twisted her wedding ring around and around her finger. "I know that my husband is considered mad by some people. Their expressions tell me so. But Heinrich is not mad. His vision makes him powerful, but not mad. He can be very difficult, I grant you, and he says many cruel things. But he does not heed what he is saying. He speaks from the fullness of his heart." She opened her hand, and began to examine it. "There is dirt under my fingernails, you see. The dirt from Troy. Sometimes I feel that I will never be free from it! It has a strange hold upon us all. It is like some accident in a life that changes everything. Yes. Troy has influenced me more than my marriage. I can say that now with confidence." She began to study her palm. "Do you hear the wind? It is gathering strength. It makes me feel ancient. Can you not hear it? If you hear anything it will be this wind." Brand made no sign, and his eyes were still open. She bent over him and met his gaze, but there was no recognition left within him.

ON THE LATE AFTERNOON, late in the day, Cyrus Redding arrived. The American consul had caught the packet-boat from Constantinople as soon as he had received the telegraph from Leonid, and he had brought with him a companion. Decimus Harding, the priest from Oxford, had been visiting him when the telegraph had been delivered.

"It was my obligation," Harding said to Sophia as they stood in the little hut. "Professor Brand would prefer the rites of the Church of England, don't you think? More suitable than the Orthodox. Besides, I wish to see Troy."

Cyrus Redding was standing with Obermann by Brand's makeshift bed. Obermann suddenly put his arm around Redding and whispered fiercely in his ear, "He cannot live."

Cyrus Redding moistened his lips and nodded. Then he turned to Harding. "It is time, sir."

Harding opened the black case he carried with him, and took out a plain wooden cross. The others moved away from the bed as he began his ministrations. As he did so, Obermann knelt down upon the floor of beaten earth and seemed to be praying fervently. When the rite had been completed, Obermann rose and, much to Harding's surprise, kissed him upon both cheeks. "I wish you to purify the house, Father Harding. From the street. Where the villagers will see you."

"There is no form of worship in the Church of England—"

"There is a rite of exorcism, is there not? Every religion has its demons."

"I do not know it by heart, I am afraid."

"Then we will improvise. Come, sir. It is the most significant and important task in this place."

"I am not in a position—"

"I am in a position. May I take your cross? Sophia, will you bring me some water from the well?"

"This is approaching blasphemy, Herr Obermann." Decimus Harding was smiling as he spoke. He seemed delighted. "I do not know if I should permit it."

"It cannot be helped. It is necessary to remove the burden from this house." Decimus Harding, Cyrus Redding and Leonid came out after him, and stood in an awkward group by the side of the path. "Come, Sophia," he said. "Do you have the water?" She had filled a small earthenware bowl from the well at the side of the road, and stood beside him.

Obermann held out the cross. "*Arma virumque cano!*" He pronounced the phrase in a voice so loud that the villagers came from the doorways, where they had been witnessing the events of the morning. "*At pius Aeneas per noctem plurima volvens.*" As he rolled out the syllables he began to sprinkle the front door and elevation of the house with water from the bowl.

"He is mixing up his Virgil," Decimus Harding whispered to Cyrus Redding. "That *is* blasphemy."

"*At regina iamdudum saucia cura!*" Obermann sprinkled the ground before the house, and then pressed the cross against the wall. "*Anna soror, quae me suspensam insomnia terrent!*"

Sophia was surprised by the actions of her husband. She realised at once that he was quoting Virgil's epic poem, and she did not wholly approve. "*At pius exsequiis Aeneas rite solutes, aggere composito tumuli, postquam alta quierunt!*" The villagers were quiet, impressed by the solemnity of the occasion, and those who inhabited the house were now embracing each other.

Obermann held up the cross once more; then, in a final gesture, he knelt down and kissed it. The villagers applauded him as he rose to his feet. He bellowed, "Purified! Purified!" *Arindi!* Then he went over to Cyrus Redding, who had been watching the ceremony in bewilderment. "We have a horse and cart for Professor Brand," he said. "We must waste no time."

"Whatever were you doing, Herr Obermann?"

"What do you think? I was exorcising the house."

"With Virgil?"

"He came to my mind. Was he not called the divine Virgil by the early Church fathers? Come. We must remove the professor while he still lives." He returned to the house and, with the help of Leonid and Sophia, he carried Brand on the straw pallet through the door and into the street. The horse and cart were tethered by the wild olive trees, and they took him over. Obermann again addressed the little crowd of villagers. "See," he said. "He is not dead! He lives!" *Olmedi! Yasiyor!*

———

THEY TRAVELLED across the plain, Obermann and Redding sitting side by side in the cart on the same bench as the driver. "No Greek or Turkish captain will carry him," Obermann explained to Cyrus Redding. "I have hired a boat that will transport us from the bay of Ezine. We will go along the coast of Marmora, stopping for provisions."

"That will take many days!"

"And how else do you suggest that we get him to Constantinople? We cannot fly. We have no magic carpet."

"He will not survive."

"In that case he must be buried at sea."

"Professor Brand is an American citizen!"

"Poseidon does not know of America, Mr. Redding. He will accept the professor."

"There are regulations." They were both speaking in low tones, as Leonid and Sophia attended to the sick man in the back of the creaking, jolting cart.

"We are not in the nineteenth century here, my dear sir. We are much further back."

"Heinrich!" Sophia called. "Heinrich! He has gone."

"He is dead? God bless him." Obermann clambered over to the body, and took up the wrist. "He has no pulse. You are right."

"He died so silently," she said. "Without a sign."

Cyrus Redding took off his straw boater. "This is a very peculiar situation," he said. "I am at a loss."

"You are with Obermann," Obermann said. "All will be well. Reverend Harding, please listen for a moment. We will proceed to the shore, where we will unload our precious burden. You may then pronounce the burial service."

"There must be an inquest, Herr Obermann." Cyrus Redding looked to Harding for support.

"And do you expect to find a coroner and a coroner's court on the plain of Troy?"

"What does the consul say to Harvard?" Harding asked Obermann. "To his relatives? I merely wish to know."

"He must say that Professor Brand died of the plague fever and that he had to be buried at once. It is common here. I will write a confirmation of this to the registry in Constantinople. If you will do the same, Reverend Harding, it will be accepted."

"What of Kadri Bey?" Sophia seemed impassive. "He will object."

"He needs to know nothing of it. The professor has left for Constantinople unexpectedly."

Harding and Redding remained silent as the horse and cart made its way slowly over the plain. When the driver came to the bay of Ezine they dismounted, one by one, on to the pebbled shore. The Aegean shimmered in the light of the late afternoon, casting a strange glow over them as they took Brand's body very carefully from the cart and laid it upon the ground.

"There is a problem," Obermann said. "If we bury him, the vultures will know of it. Even the heroes were afraid of them."

Harding gave a small shudder. "Besides," he said, "we have no spades."

"If we cannot bury him, we can burn him."

"That is not Christian, Herr Obermann."

"It is Homeric. We will light a pyre. Put him back in the cart. There is wood all around us. The boat can go on top of him." There was, in fact, much driftwood on the beach, baked dry by the sun. The boat, requisitioned by Obermann for the journey by water to Constantinople, had been hauled upon the pebbles by two fishermen who stood quietly waiting for Obermann's attention.

"You could not have planned it better." Decimus Harding seemed amused by the circumstances.

"I? I have planned nothing!"

"You misunderstand me. I mean to say that it is more fortunate than anything you could have planned."

"The gods favour us. That is all. The pyre will satisfy them. It is our tribute."

"It is very pagan, sir." Cyrus Redding was clearly unhappy with the situation.

Obermann had already gone over to the driver of the cart; he put his arm around his shoulder, and whispered to him. Immediately the driver unyoked the cart and rode off across the plain, leaving one of the horses behind. Obermann then approached the two fishermen, and began talking animatedly to them. He pointed to the sea and smoothed his hands; then he raised his arms and made great gestures towards the sky.

Leonid and Sophia walked down to the margin of the sea.

"Heinrich has planned this," she said. "I am certain of it. He knew that the professor would die on the plain."

"It is not so strange, Frau Obermann. Cremation is the ancient rite of Troy. And no Turk would bury him."

"He is unclean. Is that it?"

"There is a custom here. If a man is considered to be cursed by God, he is taken to the boundary of the town. Then he is driven away with earth and stones. When he has departed, the people turn away from him and do not look back. It is the same for Professor Brand."

The two fishermen brought the wooden cart down to the shore, and placed Brand's body within it. Then they put the boat over the corpse, and piled the cart high with driftwood.

"You will know the service by heart." Obermann had come up to Decimus Harding. "It is very English, is it not?"

"I cannot claim to recall every word, sir."

"No matter. It is of no consequence to Professor Brand. Begin, if you please. It is growing dark."

Harding went over to the cart and made the sign of the cross. "O God, through whose mercy the souls of the faithful find rest, bless, we beg Thee, this grave and place it under the care of Thy holy angel." Obermann took out a box of Lucifer matches, and applied the flame to the driftwood; it caught fire at once, and blazed around the boat. "I am the Resurrection and the Life. He that believeth in Me, even if he die he shall live. And all who live and believe in Me shall not die for ever. Shall we pray?" Cyrus Redding, Leonid and Sophia bowed their heads, as Harding intoned a half remembered prayer for the departed. As they did so, Obermann was busily poking the wood with his cane, pushing it beneath the boat so that the bier might burn more fiercely.

"Eternal rest grant unto him, O Lord. And let perpetual light shine upon him." Harding looked towards the Aegean, where the sky and sea now seemed to meet. "May the soul of the departed rest in peace. And let our cries come unto Thee."

The flames were now leaping upwards, and the heat obliged them all to step back. Then Cyrus Redding, in a surprisingly strong, clear voice, began to sing an American hymn, "The Pilgrim Comes from Lands Far Off." Obermann nodded and smiled, waving his cane in unison with the melody. "Bravo!" he cried, at the conclusion. "Bravo!"

As the sun dipped below the horizon, the sea growing darker and more turbid, they watched the funeral pyre incinerate the boat and the body of Professor Brand before sinking into ashes. Obermann shouted some instructions to the Turkish fishermen, who were able to wheel the charred cart down the pebbled shore towards the margin of the Aegean.

"Should we not scatter his ashes?" Harding asked.

"The wind will blow them back again," Obermann said. "It is better that he is entrusted to the waves."

And so the fishermen, wading into the sea, pushed the cart into the deeper parts of the water, where it slowly sank from sight, leaving a film of ash and burned wood on the surface of the sea.

"He was a charming man," Obermann said to Sophia, "but his archaeology was not perfect."

They could hear the sound of horses coming towards them, and Cyrus Redding turned in alarm.

"They are riding to your rescue," Obermann said to him. "They are your transport." The driver of the cart had returned with three horses roped together. "The reverend and the consul must ride back to Kannakale and from there take ship to Constantinople. We will go back to Hissarlik. Nothing has occurred. Nothing whatever."

"I had been hoping," Harding said, "to visit Troy. To have come so near—"

"It will remain a dream for you," Obermann replied. "I am envious. Yet you may come back. Who knows what fate may bring?"

Sophia had turned and was gazing out to sea. "Farewell, Professor. Farewell for ever." She called the words as the shadows of sea-birds passed across the water.

TWELVE

It had become unseasonably cold on the Troad plain, with sharp winds and a dawn frost clinging to the tiny red and yellow flowers scattered in profusion. The higher peaks of the Ida were covered with snow, and Obermann reported after his morning swim that the Hellespont seemed sluggish and resentful. The absence of Professor Brand had gone unremarked by the others; they had accepted Obermann's explanation that, satisfied by what he had seen at Troy, he had returned to Constantinople. "We have had the blessing of our American colleague," he said. "Now we must work on. Work is the sovereign cure! If we work, we live!" He turned to Sophia. "I have been considering what to place upon my tombstone. 'Rest in Peace. You Have Done Enough.' No. That is not quite right. Not quite the thing. This may be better. 'You Should Imitate Him. He Laboured Hard for Mortals.' It has the Greek spirit, does it not?"

She was not sure whether he was serious. "You should not think of tombs, Heinrich."

"Why not? We are surrounded by them. Who knows what is beneath our feet?" He stamped upon the ground.

He had taken up a suggestion by Sophia of clearing the area before the gates of Troy as well as the adjacent stretches of the city wall. "This is where the wooden horse once stood," she had said.

"Nothing will remain, Sophia. The horse was brought within the city."

"But I would like to see the ground on which it rested. There may have been a stone pathway. Or flat timbers may have been laid."

So they stood there, on this cold morning, looking at a square section that had been excavated to a depth of three feet. They had found pins and broken stone implements, proving that people had once trod this path, but no pavement had been uncovered. "The wooden horse has gone," Obermann said. "It served its purpose." He picked up a large stone and hurled it at a piece of scrub by the city wall. "Snake."

"How did you see it?"

"Obermann sees everything. I have told you of the brown adders?" She shook her head. "They are most deadly. If you are bitten, you will die at sunset. *Antelion.*" He seemed to be in a good humour. "The bushes of *rosa canina* conceal them. They are small, Sophia. Not larger than a worm. So beware." He started to climb the mound towards the main excavations, and Sophia was about to follow him, when Leonid came down to greet them.

"The men are very excited, Professor. An imam has told them that something glorious will be discovered today."

"Is that so, Telemachus? This holy man—does he indicate the site of this precious thing?"

"He mentioned only the ancient city. In his own words, the sun will rise once more from the old city."

"That is ingenious. But it is not exact. Nevertheless, we will work on with high hopes. We will trust the holy man."

They had been concentrating much of their excavation in the immediate vicinity of what Obermann still called Priam's palace, the stone complex at the centre of that layer which had become known as "the third city" or "the burned city." They had recently uncovered a retaining wall of brick, sixteen courses all joined with a paste made of crushed stone; above this brick construction a layer of ashes was mixed with the stones of subsequent houses, and the remnants of smaller house-walls rose again on these ruins.

Later that morning Sophia was working beside this wall, digging and sifting the debris not very far from her husband, who was trying to calculate the alignment of the entire structure.

"Heinrich," she called. "Heinrich! Here is some boring bone."

This was the phrase they had chosen to signal to one another. It was a way of avoiding the attentions of the ever alert Kadri Bey.

"Can it be left, my dear?"

"No. You must note it."

So he wandered slowly over to the trench where his wife was working. "In there," she whispered. "I see something glistening."

Obermann knelt and peered into the earth-dark cavity. He, too, thought that he had glimpsed gold.

"What time is it?" he asked Sophia.

"Almost nine o'clock."

He climbed to the top of the trench, and called out *"Paidos! Paidos!"* He knew that the men would fall to their food at once, paying no more attention to the digging than if they had been farmers eating in a neighbouring field. The call went down the line of workmen, and they dispersed on to the higher ground. Immediately he went back to the cavity and carefully extricated the copper container or utensil, about two feet long and a foot in width. There was also a large copper bowl, just behind it, which contained what seemed to be a candlestick. When Obermann moved it, however, he could see at once that it contained gold vases and cups as well as golden rings and bracelets. "Give me your shawl," he said urgently. Sophia unwound it and placed it on the ground; then, very deftly, he scooped up the golden objects from the bowl. "We must work quickly," he said. When they were all placed in the shawl, Sophia tied it and was about to hang it from the belt around her waist. "Place it within," he said. "Hitch up your skirt and put it in your underlinen."

They did not know that a small boy was watching them from a nearby trench; he was the son of one of the workmen, and was em-

ployed to carry stone away from the site in a wheelbarrow. He had lin-
gered there while the adults went to their breakfast.

"I cannot walk easily, Heinrich. Do you see the bulge?"

"No matter. Follow my direction." He put his arm about her shoulder and, with his body partially shielding the concealed gold, he led
her away from the wall to their living quarters. "If you are asked," he
whispered, "you are taken ill."

They reached their little bedroom and kitchen without being noticed. Sophia took the bundle from beneath her skirt, and was about to
pass it to Obermann when there was banging on the door. "Quick,"
he said. "Put it upon the bed and lie upon it. You are in pain."

He opened the door, and Kadri Bey stood before him. Both men
remained very calm. "What have you taken, Herr Obermann?"

"Taken? I do not understand you."

"You were seen removing some gleaming coins."

"Coins? There are no coins in Troy, Kadri Bey. You must be aware
of that."

"Something golden. The boy saw you."

"What boy?"

"The son of Hamdy."

"That boy is a notorious thief and liar. I am surprised that you allow him to remain here. His father is a cheat, also. I have repri-
manded him before."

"May I come in?"

"If you wish. Sophia has been taken ill. I pray God that it is not
the fever."

"The fever?"

"See how her body is arched. It is a sign. But come in, Kadri Bey.
I am with her. I am indifferent to personal risk." Kadri Bey remained
on the threshold. "And what has this son of a fiend said of me? I have
taken gold coins from the heart of Troy, in the middle of a hundred
workmen? It is preposterous. Come. Search my lodging, Kadri Bey.
Look everywhere in the name of the sultan. Throw open my chests
and cupboards."

"So you have found nothing at all this morning?"

"That is not precisely true. I have found some carbonised barley and a piece of petrified cheese. Do you wish to view them, Kadri Bey?"

His evident anger seemed to placate the overseer. "I will trust you, Herr Obermann. The sun must have entered the boy's eyes."

"Do not whip him. Let him go in peace. In Troy we all see things that are not real."

"My commiserations to Frau Obermann. May she recover her health."

"I pray to Allah for her, Kadri Bey. The sickness will pass."

As soon as he had gone, Obermann closed the door and locked it. "Quick," he said. "We must hide them under the floor." Sophia came from the bed, and brought over the shawl filled with gold objects. Obermann took up the floorboard in the small alcove. "God's plenty," he said, as he opened the bundle. There were gold earrings, a headband, and a sauceboat; there were two small vases with lids as well as various ornaments. "Each one of these is priceless!" He stared at them for a moment with wide eyes, and then he looked up at her. "They were hastily assembled. Why else would a bracelet be placed with a sauceboat? And they were hidden in a cavity within the wall of the palace. What does that suggest, Sophia?"

"There was some disaster."

"An impending disaster. A doom. If the Greeks had entered through the gate of Troy, that would be just such a disaster."

"If they were beating on the doors of the palace, the women would hide their treasures."

"Naturally." He picked up one of the golden vases, and examined its external markings. "Hidden for five thousand years. Does that not make you feel afraid, Sophia?"

"What is there to fear?"

"Some supernatural terror. I do not know. We have taken something from Troy. We have taken part of its secret life."

She looked at her husband in surprise. "It is too late, Heinrich."

He clenched his fist and put it up to his forehead. "Of course. It is nonsense. We have more to fear from Kadri Bey. And these treasures must be hidden again." He put them carefully in the space beneath the floor, then replaced the board. "It is their destiny to be concealed, is it not? It is the peril of gold."

"They cannot stay here, Heinrich. If we were to be absent for a few hours—"

"I know. He would come here with the eyes of Argus. But I have the solution." He did not pause, and to Sophia it seemed that the idea took shape even as he talked; he conjured it out of thin air. "Leonid and I will ride down to the sea. I will carry some satchel with me, stuffed with paper. Kadri Bey will follow us from a distance, beyond a doubt, and in his absence you must take the treasures on a journey. There is a small farm by the coast past Kannakale. I will give you the directions. Take one of the horses and ride there as quickly as you can. They will know you."

"Who are they?"

"Friends. They have proved invaluable to me in the past. So I am buying them the farm. I knew them from Ithaca."

Obermann had never mentioned these friends to her before. Once more an aspect of his life was emerging accidentally and unexpectedly. Sophia was eager to learn more about them. She had become increasingly curious about her husband's past, ever since she had learned by chance about his first wife. If he had known these suddenly revealed friends from his days on Ithaca, then they must have been involved in the excavations there. But what were they now doing upon the coast of Anatolia? And why had he agreed to buy them a farm? He had taken out a pen and paper. "You must carry this letter with you, Sophia. It will explain everything." He began writing rapidly. Then he placed the paper in an envelope, and sealed it. "I will go with Leonid in the afternoon. Be sure to wait for the departure of Kadri Bey. I will draw you a map for your journey. The place is easy to find."

"How long will it take me, Heinrich?"

"They will look after you overnight."

"You have not told me who they are."

"An old couple. Man and wife. They have no children. Here is the harbour of Kannakale." He began sketching with a pencil on a small sheet of paper. "There is a road leading east towards a village known as Karamic. It is marked. You ride down this road for a quarter of a mile. There you will find a stone hut. There is generally food and a pitcher of water left outside it. It is the home of the watcher of the sea. You know of him."

"I have never heard of him."

"Has Leonid not told you of him? I am astonished. He is a peasant who always looks out to sea. He has watched it all his life. He can do nothing else. Some say that he is blessed. Some say that he is cursed. But he looks always out to the waves and billows of the water."

"Does he speak?"

"He prays. So he is considered holy. It is said that he keeps the sea from inundating the land, as it did in previous ages. You have seen the shells in the earth about here. I almost believe in him myself. You turn right down the track that goes past his hut and travel on for half a mile. Here. I will place an X. Then you will see their farm. Their name is Skopelos."

"They are Greek?"

"Phrygian Greeks. They crossed to Ithaca from Phrygia at the time of the last famine. But they are loyal to me. I would trust them with my life. Is all this clear to you, Sophia?"

"I hope it will be safe for me to travel alone."

"You are Frau Obermann! No one will dare to touch you."

—◦◦◦—

SHE HAD DRESSED like a native woman for the journey, and her complexion was now so darkened by the sun and the wind that she did not expect to provoke much notice. For the same reason she had decided to ride upon a mule rather than a horse. She placed the golden treasures in a leather pouch, and slung it over the animal's back. Then she made her way towards the farm of the Skopeli.

THIRTEEN

It was not a hard journey. The road to Kannakale was well travelled. But she could not resist the sight of a spring a few hundred yards from the track. Partly shielded by olive trees, it was a vision of coolness and repose upon the plain. But the quietness did not last. She had come close to the water, having tethered the mule, when four black dogs hurled themselves at her furiously barking. They had come from a neighbouring vineyard. Aware of the danger, she recalled what Odysseus had done in the same situation. "As soon as the barking dogs saw Odysseus, they rushed towards him howling. Odysseus, however, wisely sat down on the ground, and let his staff slip from his hand." So she lowered herself to the earth, looking once over her shoulder to make sure that the mule was safe, and remained still. The dogs circled around her and continued to bark, but they did not touch her.

A man came running out of the vineyard, alerted by their barking, and called off the dogs. He began talking rapidly to Sophia in Turkish, but she rose to her feet and said nothing. She waved him away, making a gesture of modesty and embarrassment. He ran back to the vineyard and brought out a bunch of grapes which she accepted without a word. Then she walked back to the mule, which had remained impassive throughout Sophia's ordeal, and returned to the track. "I am pleased that I have read Homer," she said, half to herself and half to the mule.

She rode through Kannakale slowly, not wishing to draw attention to herself. And she passed unnoticed in the general noise and bustle of the town. She was relieved, however, when she had taken the road to the village of Karamic; she passed by the huts and stalls on the outskirts of Kannakale until she found herself among fields of long grass and patches of marshy ground with dunes and clumps of weed. The sky here appeared to be vast, over-arching, an infinity of pale blue that touched the earth and grassland. The sky above Troy always seemed to Sophia to be fleeting and troubled, inconstant, but here it was light and unmoved.

She recognised the hut of the watcher of the sea because, as Heinrich had predicted, there were loaves of bread and figs on the earth beside the door. She hesitated as she passed, wishing to stop and greet him. But she dared not disturb him.

She went a few yards further, then dismounted. She had promised herself, when contemplating this journey, that this was the point where she would open the envelope and read the letter that Heinrich had written in Greek to the Skopeli. She had brought a paper-knife with her for that purpose, and she easily unsealed the vellum envelope that Obermann always used for his correspondence. The preliminary greetings were followed by a passage that Obermann had underlined:

> I am sorry to inform you that we are closely watched and expect that the Turkish overseer, who is angry with me, I do not know for what reason, will search our house tomorrow. I therefore deposit with you certain articles, knowing that you will lock them up and hide them where no Turk will be able to touch them or discover them. The villagers betray me to the Turk so that I cannot use their horses. When I come to remove these articles have ready for me three horses in the night. Farewell. Sophia, the wife of whom I have told you, does not know the history.

What did this mean? "Sophia does not know the history"? To her, this meant a tale or a story. What story did she not know? And was this not a curt and impersonal way of describing her? To her surprise, she felt anger rather than curiosity. In some way he had betrayed her to strangers. She did not know the nature of that betrayal, as she did not know so many things, but she feared it. And she was indignant. She had no conception of what the story might be, but she guessed that it was a dark one.

The watcher of the sea came out of his stone hut, and took up a pitcher of water that had been left on the threshold. He did not seem to notice Sophia, although she was standing close to him by the side of the path. She deliberately sought out his eyes, but they registered no impression of her presence. They were bright, but they seemed blank. Was it possible to suffer from sea-blindness? He went back into his hut. He reappeared after a few moments and retrieved the loaves of bread, again without giving any sign that he had seen her. In truth he still saw the sea.

She placed the letter back in its envelope and resealed it, making sure that she smeared dust upon the back as if it had fallen into the road. Then she continued her journey. Fifteen minutes later, she reached the farm. The one-storeyed house was built upon the standard pattern of this countryside, with walls of large clay bricks; the roof was constructed with flat boards, on which was heaped a thick layer of clay as protection against the rain. But it was an unusually large house, with a wooden porch running in front it. There were also several barns and outbuildings, which gave the appearance of prosperity.

No one was in sight, but Sophia could faintly hear a woman singing. She called out, and the singing stopped at once. A man stepped on to the porch and asked her in Turkish what she wanted. "I am the wife of Heinrich Obermann," she said. "Sophia."

He held out his arms to her. "Of course. Welcome." He spoke in Greek to her. "He has told us about you. Maria! Quickly!" A woman came on to the porch and put her hand up to her eyes as if shielding them from the sun. "It is Sophia. He has sent her."

The husband and wife made a marked contrast. He was a full and ample man, with fleshy face and large limbs; she was much thinner, much smaller, and beside him seemed almost insubstantial. She took a step back, in surprise, and with a nervous gesture smoothed her hair with her hands.

"You honour us," he said. "Come in. Maria, prepare for our guest." Maria went back quickly into the house. "I am Theodore," he said.

"I am a messenger from my husband. He sends you this." She took out the letter and, as Skopelos was reading it, she went over to the mule and untied the leather pouch that held the golden vessels and ornaments. When she brought the pouch over to him, he accepted it without a word, almost solemnly, and carried it into one of the out-buildings.

The yard was quiet. For a successful farm, there was very little sign of activity. As she stood beside the mule, she could hear Maria—she supposed it was Maria—talking quickly and animatedly. She must have been instructing a servant, since there was no reply. She detected a slight querulousness in her voice and decided, on a sudden instinct, that she did not wish to stay in this place overnight.

Theodore came out of the barn, smiling. "Allow me to take you inside," he said. "My wife will wish to feed you."

The interior was somewhat dark, with blinds drawn against the afternoon sun, and it was dominated by some large and elaborate pieces of ebony furniture. There was an icon of the Virgin upon one wall, with three candles placed in saucers before it. Maria came in, bearing a tray of small cakes covered with sugar powder like dust. "Eat," she said. "Eat after your long journey."

Sophia knew well the laws of host and guest, and could not refuse the offering.

"How is he?" Theodore asked her. "Is he well?"

"My husband is flourishing. You have seen Troy?"

"Oh, no. We do not bother him at his work. He is too busy. We hear from him from time to time."

"You met my husband in Ithaca?"

"Many years ago. We performed some slight services for him, and he has been kind."

Sophia would have liked to have learned more about these "services," but he had fallen silent.

"You farmed there?" she asked him.

"No. We owned a guest-house."

"A hotel?"

"A very small affair. There were foreigners coming to our island in the footsteps of Odysseus. English. French. German. I guided them."

"And that is how you met my husband."

"Except that he guided me. He is a great expert on Ithaca."

Sophia sipped the strong tea that Maria had brewed for her.

"How is Leonid?" Theodore asked her.

"You know Leonid?"

"Of course."

"He is a good boy," Maria said. She had a thin, plaintive voice. "He prays before the Virgin." She looked towards the icon, and touched her breast.

Sophia was surprised that they knew Leonid, and that he should come to this place. Did he bring money from Heinrich? Or did he transport other treasures for them to hide?

"Do you have neighbours?" she asked them.

"They leave us alone," Theodore replied. "There is space enough for everyone here."

"But you are Greeks among Turks."

"They do not harm us. We are quiet people, as you can see, and keep to ourselves."

"My husband says that you come from Phrygia."

"Ah yes. We are closer to it here. And the landscape reminds us of it. The plain. The distant mountains—"

"Why do you not go back?"

"That is an interesting question. We have duties. Responsibilities. We love your husband. You must have more tea—"

There was silence between them. "What do you grow here?"

"We grow enough to live. We have a little surplus that we sell. We are content. We are simple people."

Sophia did not believe them to be simple at all. Indeed she was more puzzled by them now than before she had met them. "But you have a servant."

"A servant?" Maria seemed surprised.

"I heard you talking to her."

"Oh. A girl. An orphan girl who works in the kitchen. But she will not disturb you."

"She would not disturb me in the least. She has a strong voice for a child."

"I do not understand," Maria said.

"I heard her singing when I arrived."

"You did? She has gone now. She has gone into the fields."

There was a further silence.

"I must leave you both," Sophia said eventually.

"Will you not stay for the night?"

"No. Thank you. I must go back while it is still light."

They made no further effort to persuade her to stay, so she rose from the large ebony chair. Then she fell back.

—◆—

SHE AWOKE the following morning, fully clothed, lying upon an ornate bed in a small whitewashed room. She had been woken by a knock upon the door. Maria came in with two eggs and a wheaten loaf. "You were very tired after your journey," she said. "You fell asleep."

"I must have fainted—"

"No. You slept very deeply. That is all."

Sophia knew that the atmosphere of the plain was supposed to be soporific, but it had never affected her before so suddenly or so powerfully.

"Leonid is here," Maria said.

"Leonid?"

"He will accompany you home. He is a good boy."

After Sophia had washed her hands and face in the porcelain bowl provided for her, she left the room and found Leonid sitting on the porch. He was talking quietly and seriously to Theodore, but, as soon as he saw Sophia, he rose and smiled. "Greetings, Frau Obermann. I hear that you slept well."

"It is the air."

"I know it. It is unusual here."

She had brought out her eggs, so eager was she to see Leonid, and came over to the porch. "I had not expected you. Would you care for an egg?"

"No, thank you, I have eaten already. It is a long journey for you alone. The professor regretted asking you—but there was no one else."

"And Kadri Bey suspected nothing?"

"It was wonderful!" Leonid clapped his hands. "The professor and I rode across the plain to the Aegean, not wishing to look back, and when we came to the bay at Granica we dismounted. We could hear the faint beat of hooves somewhere in the distance, so we knew that they were following us. We waited until we felt their presence among the rocks above us. On the plain you can sense other human beings without seeing them. That was how it was. Then we stripped, leaving our clothes and our satchels upon the shore, and plunged into the sea. We swam to the little promontory outside the bay, and hid ourselves. We watched as Kadri Bey and his two men came down to the shore, searched our satchels—searched our horses—searched the area around us—and then retreated to the rocks utterly baffled and defeated. They had seen us enter the Aegean quite naked, and re-alised that we could have taken nothing. The professor was joyous."

"How did you explain my absence when you returned to Troy?"

"You are not absent. You are lying in a fever, where no one will dare to disturb you. When we go back, I will say that you have taken the air for a few minutes."

"I am ready now," she said. She did not wish to stay on the farm for longer than was necessary.

"Good. You are quite composed?"

"Of course."

"Before we go I must show you Ferdinand." He stepped over to Theodore, and said something to him.

"He is in the field," Theodore said. "Come this way."

Sophia and Leonid followed him past the outbuildings; she glanced into the one where he had taken the treasures, but it was empty with a floor of beaten earth. They came on to a field where a large white goat was grazing on the lush grasses. "Ferdinand! Ferdinand!" Theodore was calling to it, and the goat began to amble towards him. Sophia noticed that its legs were longer than those of the goats of Greece. Then Theodore took a pipe or flute from the pocket of his shirt, and began to play a soft, slow melody. The goat stood upon its hind legs, as the music played, and began to dance. Sophia could think of no other word. It performed a dance in front of her, its forelegs bent gracefully. It turned in a circle, against the background of the distant mountains.

"It is not trained," Leonid told her. "It dances quite naturally." Theodore put down his pipes, and the goat resumed its grazing. "Frau Obermann and I must go back to Troy, Theodore. We thank you."

They returned to the main house where Maria was waiting for them. Leonid embraced Maria warmly, kissing her on both cheeks, and she held on to him very tightly. Then he embraced Theodore, and patted him on the back. Sophia remained apart from them, but Maria approached her and kissed her hand. "You are always a friend," she said.

"I am glad of it."

Theodore brought out her mule, which had been fed and brushed down, and Leonid untethered his horse from a post in the yard. *"Khairete!"* they cried. *"Khairete!"*

They had ridden some two or three hundred yards, savouring the freshness of the morning air, when they heard a scream, abject, hysterical, helpless. It came from the farmhouse. Sophia looked back in alarm, but Leonid gave no response. "It is the goat invading the kitchen," he said. "After dancing it does that." Then he added, "Maria always screams."

They rode on, and came within sight of the stone hut owned by the watcher of the sea.

"How long have they known my husband?"

"Many years."

"And they followed him to Troy."

"They consider him to be their patron. Their guardian, if you will."

"He gives them money."

"He supports them. The professor is generous."

"And in return?"

"They do little services for him. Like this one."

"They hide certain objects?"

"That is a way of putting it. They preserve objects that would otherwise be scattered to the winds. The professor wishes to build a great museum of antiquity, where all his discoveries may be seen in one place. He does not want to leave pieces of Troy in Constantinople or in Paris."

Sophia had no knowledge of any Obermann museum, but she managed to conceal her surprise. "He has told me of the house in Athens. My father has agreed to help him."

"Yes. That is so. It should make you proud, Frau Obermann. The professor wishes to build his museum in the heart of your own city. It will be a tribute to Homer himself."

Yet for some reason Sophia felt no comfort in this, as they made their way back across the plain.

———〜〜〜———

SOPHIA FOUND her husband lying on the floor of their dwelling. He was holding a ceramic bowl and gently stroking it. It seemed to her that he had been whispering to it.

"Tell me about the Skopeli," she said.

"They work for me."

"I thought them mysterious."

"The Phrygian is secretive by nature. Even when he has no secret worth speaking of."

"They have a dancing goat."

"A mad animal. I do not approve of madness." And he said no more upon the subject.

FOURTEEN

Obermann was kneeling upon the hard ground. "I thank the gods that I have lived until this day." Then he bent over and kissed a large grey stone. "The world will now be changed."

They had been excavating, in the weeks after the discovery of the golden treasures, in the vicinity of the palace. Some grains and seeds had been found; these were duly collected and registered, as well as some fragments of pottery and a strange row of leaden balls that seemed to form a system of weights. And then one of the workmen noticed the flat grey stones: they were scattered across the layer of ground just excavated, and at first they were ignored or pushed aside as natural debris. But then Sophia noticed a curious nick or cut in the side of one. When she picked it up she realised that it was lighter than any stone and of a different texture; she brushed away the soil with her forefinger and, to her surprise, she uncovered a row of curious markings on the flat upper surface. She put it down very carefully on the side of the trench, and picked up another. A similar row of signs or marks had been incised upon its surface. She had no conception of what these markings might be, so she sat down upon a low stone wall by the edge of the trench and stared at them. As far as she could tell they were not random lines: there were curves and diagonals, dots and parallel bars, but all in apparent sequence. Then, in the first stage of understanding, she almost dropped the tablet. Her hands began to tremble, and she placed it beside her. Her throat became dry. She got up carefully, and walked over to Leonid and her husband, who were standing together near the old palace wall. "Heinrich," she said, "Heinrich. I have found an object that may interest you."

Something in her voice arrested Obermann's attention. He turned towards her slowly. "Yes, my dear?"

"I have found some inscriptions."

"There are no inscriptions in Troy."

"Markings, then. Human markings. I am sure of it."

"Well, let us see these markings."

They walked over to the side of the trench where Sophia had been working. She pointed to the flat tablet that she had left upon the wall. Leonid picked it up very gently, and proceeded to study it. "I do not know what to say, Professor. I have seen nothing like it."

Obermann held out his hands, and Leonid placed it carefully within them. He bent his head low over it, as if he were about to smell it or taste it. He was still for a few moments and, when he raised his head, Sophia noticed that tears were welling from his eyes. "Where did you find this, Sophia?"

"Here. There are many of them, scattered across the ground. But they are not stones, Heinrich."

"No. They are not stones. They are tablets of clay. They have been baked in some great fire." He was talking very slowly and distinctly. "Do you know what they are, Sophia? They are writing tablets. They are pages."

"There was no writing in Troy, Professor. The dates—"

"There was writing in Troy, Telemachus. This is the writing in Troy. Their words. Their language. After three thousand years of silence, they are speaking to us again."

They gathered up the clay tablets that afternoon, but Obermann was very quiet. He seemed distracted and uncertain. When Sophia asked him if he was in low spirits, he smiled at her. "Not at all. It is simply that I cannot fathom this as yet. I am at a loss." Lineau came into the hut where the tablets were being kept. "Ah. Here is the man who sees what we cannot see. Sit, Monsieur Lineau. I will give you a wonderful thing."

Lineau ran the fingers of his right hand quickly over the tablet that Obermann had offered to him. "The marks have been cut with a stylus or some other sharp point into the clay," he said. "They have been incised cleanly and efficiently. There is no hesitation. These are not hieroglyphs, Herr Obermann. They are not pictographs."

"Not Egyptian?"

"Far from it. The symbols go in linear progression. Do you see the straight lines that divide one row of symbols from another? This is a form of linear writing. I have never come upon it before." He turned his face towards Obermann. "Of all the treasures we have found in Troy this is by far the greatest. You will not be able to hide it from the Turks."

"I have no intention of doing so, Monsieur Lineau. I have already informed Kadri Bey. Our overseer has jumped in the air, as if he were a cow in the moon."

"A cow over the moon, Heinrich."

"And has rushed to telegraph Constantinople. I still cannot believe it myself. And here comes the potentate."

Kadri Bey had joined them. "I was not sure how to describe them," he said. "I have merely said that they are tablets of writing."

"Here. Gaze upon them, Kadri Bey, and marvel." The overseer looked at them, keenly enough, but he did not touch them. "They are the earliest examples of writing in Europe."

"We are not in Europe, Herr Obermann. We are in Turkey."

"Such is the narrow view, Kadri Bey. But this is Troy. This is the land of the Greeks. Of Hector and of Priam."

"It has yet to be proved."

"Proved? The poems of Homer prove it beyond any reasonable doubt!" He took up one of the tablets. "Here are their first words. They are speaking to us across the abysm of time. I see them on the further shore—" He broke off and turned towards his wife. "I must not cry before these gentlemen, Sophia. You will scold me. You will accuse me of acting out some drama."

"I will accuse you of nothing, Heinrich, except love for Troy."

"I know it. And Kadri Bey shares that love with me, do you not?"

"As long as Troy remains in Turkey."

Lineau was still tracing out the tablet with his fingers. "There is no one in the world who will be able to interpret these signs," he said. "They are unlike any other."

"Do not lose heart at the beginning, Monsieur Lineau. We have an incalculable advantage. We know them to be Greek."

"Thousands of years will separate these marks from the words of Homer. I do not know that we can even use the word Greek to describe them."

"And what word would you choose?"

"I have no notion."

"So be it. We will call them No Texts from No Town in Nowhere." He relented his tone. "Forgive me, Lineau. I am overexcited, as you can see. I do not think I will sleep for the rest of my life. We should be brave. Adventurous. Why should we not be able to interpret these symbols? If we assume it to be Greek, as I insist on doing, the words will slowly reveal their meaning to us. The dead will speak."

—◊◊◊—

THE MUSEUM OF ANTIQUITIES in Constantinople, informed of Kadri Bey's message by telegraph, instructed Obermann to take the utmost care of the tablets, to store them, and to await further instructions. The director of the museum had in the meantime been in contact with his counterpart, Augustus Franks, at the British Museum in London, where an entirely new department devoted to Proto-historical Scripts had recently been established. It was agreed between the two directors that a brilliant young member of the new team, Alexander Thornton, would journey with all speed to Hissarlik.

"He will be some drone of the museum," Obermann said to Sophia. "Some pale Englishman. I know the English very well. They are either bullies or cowards. Or they are hypocrites. Like our friend, the Reverend Harding. Is Harding the man to bring Christianity to the Turks? He would turn the people of Oxford into pagans." He took off his hat and fanned his face with it. "I wonder what kind of Englishman Mr. Thornton will turn out to be."

FIFTEEN

Alexander Thornton arrived three weeks later, after a journey by sea from Tilbury. He did not seem to Sophia to be a museum drone, as her husband had anticipated; he looked to her more like an athlete or a mountaineer. He was tall and very slim, with a distinct tan after his weeks at sea.

Kadri Bey insisted on welcoming him to the site of Troy with elaborate courtesies. Sophia watched the young man carefully, almost eagerly, as he shook hands and bowed and tasted the little cup of Turkish coffee presented to him. He was not awkward, but he was precise and restrained in manner. "I hope I find you well, sir," he said to Obermann.

"I have never been so well in my life, Mr. Thornton. I flourish."

"I am glad of it, sir. In England we have all heard of your great work. And now this—"

"You will see my great work soon, Mr. Thornton. Permit me to introduce you to Frau Obermann."

"Delighted." He gave a small bow before taking her hand, but he could not conceal his surprise at finding a female in the middle of the excavations.

Obermann laughed, and slapped him on the back. "You do not think this a suitable place for a woman?"

"On the contrary. I am delighted."

"Spoken like an Englishman. What did I tell you, Sophia? They are always fair. Did you know, Mr. Thornton, that you are standing on the precise spot where the wooden horse of the Greeks was once placed?"

"It is an honour, I am sure. But I always believed that the story of the horse was simply that—a story."

"You have been in the British Museum too long, Mr. Thornton. You have lost your sense of wonder."

"I joined the museum six months ago, sir. You must not blame my shortcomings upon it. They are all my own."

———

THORNTON WAS INDEED accustomed to making judgements for himself. His mother had died, of a cancer, when he was fifteen years old; from that time forward he had become more thoughtful and self-reliant. He started to question the world. More particularly he had begun to question the society all around him. He had decided to study theology at Oxford because he wished to become a pastor in the East End of London, where he could minister to the poor and outcast of that region. Then, on one of his long walks into the countryside around Oxford, he became uneasy about the principles of the Church in which he had been raised. And, eventually, doubt put out his faith. He abandoned theology, and took up the relatively new study of palaeography in the Department of Archaeology at the university. But he had not lost his concern for social justice. He joined the City Education League, and became an advocate of advanced thinking on workers' rights and the female cause. He had even given lectures on reform at Exeter Hall.

———

"YOU ARE A MAN of spirit," Obermann was saying. "I applaud you."

Sophia had been watching Thornton throughout their exchange. He seemed wary, thoughtful, but she sensed some hidden amusement on his part at her husband's manner. She was not sure if she liked this or not. "Mr. Thornton would like to see his quarters, Heinrich," she said. "He has travelled far."

"I am afraid, Mr. Thornton, we do not have golden bowls of water or serving maidens. We are not yet Homeric here. We try our hardest, but we fall short of the poet's standards."

"I would really wish to see the subject as soon as possible."

"I beg your pardon?"

"The subject. The tablets. That is why I have come."

"You are in a great hurry, Mr. Thornton. But I admire that. I revere it. In every situation of my life I have always proved how much a person can accomplish with iron will. I myself was secretly circumcised in Mecca so that I might better escape detection!" Sophia looked at her husband strangely. Why did he lie about so private a matter? "So. We will take you to your subject." He led him to the hut where the tablets were kept. "They are stored here," he said. "It is a good dry place. They are snug, as you say in England."

When Thornton came into the room he was very alert. "I had not expected so great a number," he said.

"We have one hundred and seventy-eight separate objects. They are of approximately the same size and appearance, as you can see. But, of course, the markings are quite different on each of them."

"There will be patterns and repeated motifs," Thornton replied. "May I?" He picked up one of the tablets, and scrutinised it with a look of surprise and abstraction. Sophia wondered if he were not short-sighted, so closely did he hold it to his face; she also noticed that his hands were trembling slightly. "May I ask you this, Herr Obermann? What is your guess about the languages spoken in this region of the world? I have heard various opinions."

"They belonged to the Indo-European stock, but they were as different from one another as Latin is from Greek. I doubt whether Albanian can be classified as an Aryan language at all."

"But they were not Semitic?"

"It is very doubtful. It is my belief that the language spoken in this city was ancient Illyrian or Thracian."

"Is that not the same as Pelasgian?"

"I am amazed at your knowledge, sir."

"It is my profession. But then Homer uses the term to describe the Achaean Greeks, not the Thracians themselves." He was still looking very closely at the tablets. "They are a kind of baked clay bar but rather like a stone chisel in shape." It was as if he were talking to himself. "They are broken at one end. There is a script and what appear to be numerals. They were engraved on the wet clay and are evidently the work of practised scribes. No doubt you have reached the same conclusions, sir."

"Precisely the same, Mr. Thornton."

"And do you have an estimate of the date?"

"They were found at the level of the burned city of Troy, and so I estimate that they were produced around 1800 B.C."

"You are very precise."

"That is *my* profession."

"It is an early date for writing of this nature. Assuming it to be Indo-European."

"The date will be universally adopted. I feel sure of it." Thornton looked at him with the veiled air of amusement that Sophia had already noticed. "My first impressions are never wrong, Mr. Thornton. Do you know what an archaeologist must possess?"

"A knowledge of geometry?"

"You are a Pythagorean! No. The archaeologist must have inspiration. Vision. Imagination. May I tell you a story? When we were digging in Ithaca we found no source of water. The palace of Odysseus must have contained wells, but what had become of them? Covered with the silt of the centuries. My men wished to sink a new well in a corner of the courtyard, but I knew them to be mistaken. Acting on an inference from the contour of the hillside above—are you following me, Mr. Thornton?—I drew a cross in the earth beside a large block that happened to be standing at that spot and ordered them to dig there. Then I went off on a journey. When I came back, the world was agog!"

"What had happened, sir?"

"My workmen had taken off no more than fifteen inches of the top soil before they uncovered the choked opening of an ancient well, some three feet in diameter. It is the same well of which Homer writes, with its clear spring! At the bottom, thirty feet down, there was an abundant spring of water that proved to be of better quality than any for miles around. It is still in use among the people of Ithaca, who bless me every morning in their prayers. And that was not the end of it. Beside the well we unearthed a pair of two-handled pitchers, for which we found a use immediately. That is archaeology, Mr. Thornton."

"It is a very impressive story."

"Of course, my men considered my mark—my cross—to be a sign of supernatural guidance and hailed me as a man of miracles."

"I do not doubt it."

"I did not contradict them. That is what I mean by inspiration."

Sophia had heard this story before, but she was sure that her husband had spoken of Tiryns rather than of Ithaca. "I expect that Mr. Thornton would like to see his quarters now," she said.

"I confess to being tired."

"But you may plead my husband in your defence. He has tired whole armies of men with his stories."

"Mr. Thornton is inspired, Sophia. He wishes to close his eyes and dream of Troy. We have all done it."

"I hardly ever dream." He looked at Sophia. "But I would be grateful for a bed."

She took him toward the small enclosure that held their huts and cottages. "It *is* surprising," he said, "to find a female here. If you permit me to say so."

"You may say what you like, Mr. Thornton. This is a place of freedom." She laughed. "But I am not the only female here. We have many Turkish women working beside the men. We find that all work better when they are together."

"I am glad to hear of it. I believe that the sexes should be equal in the business of life."

She glanced at him for a moment, and noticed his serious—almost determined—expression. "You believe in this equality?"

"Oh, yes. I have spoken on the subject in Exeter Hall."

"I am afraid such theories have not yet reached Greece."

"But they have reached your husband surely. He makes you a partner in his labours. He allows you to escort me to my quarters."

"He is very good."

"No, not good. Enlightened. We have need of more men like him in England. Do you know that they will not employ women in the museum? It is a scandal."

Once more she noticed his earnestness. "The divinity of this place is a woman," she said. "Athene Glaucopis."

"I know."

"Her epithet means that her eyes lighten through the night. She sees us as we sleep. She watches over us. But you do not need protecting, Mr. Thornton. You say that you do not dream."

"Are dreams so dangerous, then?"

"Of course. A dream can affect your physical health. I have often discussed this with my husband. He loves to dream. He says that dreams give him strength."

"And you?"

"Oh, I close my eyes and I see visions. I see streams and rivers and trees. I summon them up. I wish for them. And they appear. It is one of the great comforts of my life." She wondered if she had become too confiding. "And in dreams come prophecies and warnings."

"You believe this?"

"You will believe it, too. When you have stayed at Troy. Here are your quarters." His was a stone hut, built from the stones of Troy itself, with a roof of thatch. After the unhappy presence of William Brand, Obermann's guests were no longer welcome in the village. "You must prepare yourself for the wind. Somehow it will manage to find its way through these stones and sing to you."

"This is tremendous. These are the very stones from the excavations, are they not? I feel honoured to be protected by them. They are very reassuring."

"They are strong and fierce. The pitcher and basin are there. And what my husband calls the unmentionable is beneath the bed. We go down to the river for our complete ablutions. There is a place for men and a place for women, which are marked very clearly. You know of mealtimes already."

He was only half listening. "Do you think I may move the clay tablets here?"

"You must ask my husband. Do you believe that, beside the old stones themselves, they will speak to you?"

"No. Not at all. I like to begin my work at the earliest possible time. My mind is clearest at dawn. When the world awakes, so do I."

He seemed to Sophia to be the strangest mixture of romance and practicality. With his impossible hopes for women, he was clearly a dreamer; yet he professed not to dream. He was scholarly and thoroughly practical about the tablets, yet he was thrilled to be surrounded by the stones of Troy. He would bear further observation.

SIXTEEN

On the following morning Alexander Thornton started work upon the clay tablets. He had with him a magnifying glass, a large notebook and a number of pens. "The nibs are shaped differently," he told Obermann, "so that I can copy the symbols exactly." He asked if the tablets could be taken to his quarters, and Obermann readily agreed. So he carefully placed twenty or more in a wheelbarrow and took them to his stone hut, repeating the operation until all had been safely removed. Then he put the tablets in rows upon the floor, and began the work of copying each one. He noticed at once that they were a combination of symbols and of pictures. There was a dagger and a bowl, a wheel and a horse's head; there was an amphora, and a one-handled goblet. He drew these very slowly, exactly imitating the curves and dots of the clay originals. The horse's head reminded him of the white horse cut into the chalk of the valley at Uffington; it had a similar quality of spirited life. While he was an undergraduate at Oxford he had tramped to that valley, along the banks of the Thames, and could still recall the sensation of wonder at the first sight of the great beast springing out of the earth. He experienced the same wonder now.

Other pictograms were less easy to decipher. One was of an oval structure placed upon a wheel but, as he drew it, he realised that it was a chariot. Another shape was probably that of a cloth or tunic, and there seemed to be a horned creature resembling an ox. But some signs could only have been words, or letters, or syllables; there were dots and short lines that could only be numbers, as far as Thornton could tell. Some symbols were repeated, and some appeared on several of the clay tablets. Yet who could break their silence now, with the scribes and the city itself long buried under the dust of ages? The tablets were spread over so large an area of the floor that there was scarcely room for him to tread. But he liked to sleep among them; he liked to wake in the morning, when they were the first elements of the world that he saw. The drawings he had made were now hanging by strings from the crude wooden rafters of the roof. He had tried to arrange them in vertical rows, where the same sign or set of signs could be seen; he believed that, if he lived with them long enough, the so far invisible correspondences and associations would become clearer to him. And, on staring at the clay tablets from his bed, immediately after waking, he hoped that he would be able to detect affinities between them.

His first impression was that they did not represent an Indo-European language at all; the signs seemed to him to be too stark or, as he put it to himself, "too alien." He had no conclusive proof, of course, but the system of writing seemed closer to that of the Egyptians or the Assyrians. This would confound Obermann's theory that the inhabitants of Troy spoke an early form of Greek, but he was sure that he could persuade him of the truth of the matter. Truth was above all prejudice and wishful thinking. But he would have to labour harder, and longer, before he could even tentatively suggest such conclusions. He might, in any case, prove to be entirely wrong.

———

SOPHIA KNOCKED upon his door, to tell him that lunch was ready; she would have walked away, but Thornton called her in. "Forgive the muddle," he said. "It is no muddle to me but—"

"But a woman's sense of tidiness would consider it so. I agree with you, Mr. Thornton."

"Oh, no. Nothing of the kind. To anyone else at all, it would seem like chaos." He had rearranged the tablets in vertical rather than horizontal fashion, and his pallet bed was covered with slips of paper upon which he had drawn the pictograms. "I wished to show you this, Mrs. Obermann."

"You have been here two days, Mr. Thornton. You have earned the right to call me Sophia. We are in Troy, not in London. And, if I may, I will call you Alexander. Shall we make a pact on it?"

"Of course. Yes. I would be delighted. I call Leonid by his first name, after all. And I have almost called Lineau Pierre." Sophia had always judged people by the way in which they laughed, and Thornton had a singularly charming expression. "Except I do not know how he would react. He seems to be of the old fashion."

"You mistake him, Alexander. Monsieur Lineau is always talking to me of the new methods of discovery."

He had gone over to the bed and snatched up a slip of paper. "This is what I wanted to show you. Do you see these two figures, on separate lines? Do you see a resemblance between them?"

"A very strong one."

"What does each one suggest to you?"

"A toasting-fork?"

"Look again. A line with a curve or hook at its top. Then it is bisected with one line on either side. Do you see? Then two lines come down. This is where the difference lies."

"In one figure the lower lines cross, and in the other they move apart from each other."

"Do you not see it? It is a human figure."

"Now that you say it, I see it."

"That is always the way."

"The head. The arms. The legs. Yet why the difference in the legs?"

"The figure with the legs crossed is the man. The other is the woman."

"How can you be sure of that?"

"The figure of the man appears much more often than that of the woman. It is common sense."

"But you are an idealist, Alexander." She enjoyed using his first name. "Can you not imagine a society in which women were predominant?"

"We have only the legend of the Amazons, I am afraid. I am convinced, too, that crossed legs were a sign of power and authority. It may be that the king or chieftain crossed his legs when he sat upon his throne. So it became a symbol of the male."

"And the woman is open. Ready to receive."

"Yes." He seemed embarrassed. "That is so."

"The male is closed off. Ready to strike."

"You see more than I do, Mrs. Obermann. Sophia."

"But now that I have seen it, it is there. What is this symbol here?"

"This puzzles me. It is like an arrow pushing against an horizontal line. But if that line were the surface of the ground, then the arrow might represent wheat growing out of the earth. You see, here is a shape like barley, coming out of the same horizontal line as if it had grown. But this is a guess." They were bent over the tablet, their heads almost touching, when they heard the voice of Obermann.

"Lunch waits for no man, Mr. Thornton." He was standing in the doorway. "You detain our guest, Sophia."

"Alexander was telling me his deductions. They are fascinating."

"I look forward to hearing them from Alexander." He emphasised the name. "Lunch is served."

Over the meal Obermann was recollecting a journey to Bosnia he had undertaken three years before in search of antiquities. "I had an English companion with me. Have you heard of Arthur Mackenzie, Mr. Thornton?" Thornton shook his head. "A first-rate geologist. Feeling rather thirsty, after a long walk south from Sarajevo, he called for water in the first village we passed. At once, without more words, a small boy took us over to the village spring. The Slavonic word for 'water' is '*wada.*' Then we discovered that their word for 'milk' is '*mlieke.*' This is no coincidence, Mr. Thornton." Obermann was addressing all his remarks towards the Englishman; it seemed to Sophia that he was challenging him.

"It is no coincidence at all, Herr Obermann. The Slav and the Englishman have a common ancestor, many thousands of years before. I believe our forefathers came from the highlands of central Asia. We are all part of the same stock of Indo-Europeans."

"Just as my Trojans are."

"That is a difficult point to resolve."

"No matter. No matter." He waved it away. "When I was in Bosnia I was often addressed as '*brat,*' or brother, and the Bosnians are known to call the stranger '*shija,*' or neighbour. Do you know why they have this egalitarian spirit? I am sorry to say it, Kadri Bey, but they consider their Turkish masters to be despots. They are united in communal spirit."

"We are not unjust, Herr Obermann. We have caused less unrest and suffering than the British Empire."

"I do not think that Mr. Thornton will agree with you, Kadri Bey."

"On the contrary. My country has been guilty of great wrongs."

"You are an unusual Englishman," Kadri Bey replied.

"I think, sir, that in this place we are all unusual."

"Well put." Obermann laughed and clapped his hands. "We are all beasts in Troy. We are all wooden horses!"

"The British Empire," Lineau said, "has produced some fearless men. I worked once with Henry Rawlinson."

"You knew him?" Thornton was incredulous. "He is my hero. I revere him."

"He still lives, Mr. Thornton."

"A hero can be living," Obermann said.

"I worked with him in Persia." Lineau ignored Obermann's interruption. "When he was British minister there. He was burdened with political affairs, but he never lost his passion for antiquity."

"Who is Rawlinson?" Sophia asked her husband.

"Have you never heard of him? He introduced the world to Babylon and to Persia. He was a voyager through the seas of thought. Is that not so, Mr. Thornton?" Lineau continued still, taken up by his theme. "When he was a young officer he had the good fortune to be posted to Kermanshah within the Zagros Mountains."

"There were brigands there," Obermann told his wife. "It was wild and trackless. It had lost its past."

"Not quite," Lineau said. "Rawlinson was stationed a few miles from a place called Bisitun. It is a great stone rock, hundreds of feet in height, in the foothills of the Zagros range. It is on the broad highway between Ecbatana and Babylon. The King of Persia, Darius, the King of Kings, ordered that a vast image of himself be carved high upon the face of the rock, with his enemies at his feet. At the foot of this rock is a clear spring, very cold to the touch. There is a pool here where the local people bring their offerings. It is considered to be a place of God." Lineau's blind eyes were moving rapidly from side to side. "Together with the image of the king is a long inscription written in three different tongues. Then Darius ordered that his workmen should smooth the face of the rock so that no one might climb up and deface the great work. And so it was."

"Rawlinson was an adventurer," Obermann said. "He climbed."

"He copied the inscriptions," Lineau went on. "Then, little by little, he began to decipher them. They were in Babylonian, in Old Persian and in a strange tongue known as Elamite. Their writing is known as cuneiform. Wedge-shaped letters. The earliest of all human words."

"It was a wonderful feat of decipherment," Thornton said. "It rivals Champollion and the Egyptian hieroglyphics."

"Such energy. Such agility." Obermann was silent for a moment. "But that is not enough for us. Now that Mr. Thornton speaks of rivalry, we must rival Rawlinson. We must decipher the language of Troy. Surely that will be the greatest feat of all!"

"It is interesting," Thornton said, "that the language of the Persians and the Babylonians was Semitic."

"The Trojans were not Semites. They were part of Indo-European stock. I know it."

"What do you know, Herr Obermann?" Thornton asked. "I mean, what do you truly know?"

"I know myself, as the Greeks have it. I know when I am correct."

"That is a great gift."

"The Semites come from Mesopotamia. What has Troy to do with the sons of Shem? The Trojans belong to western Asia and the Indo-European languages. That is why we are so close to them."

"But what if we were not so close?" Thornton asked Obermann. "What if they were more mysterious and alien than we realise?"

"I cite you the evidence of Homer."

"What if Homer had nothing to do with them?"

"Nonsense, Mr. Thornton. Alexander." He may have suggested the slightest mockery, but he turned at once to Sophia. "Mr. Thornton is becoming a heretic, Sophia. You must convert him before he is burned."

"He must speculate on all possibilities, Heinrich. That is why you value him so highly."

"Of course. I forget. But tell me this. How is it that this landscape around us thoroughly agrees with the descriptions in Homer's poem?"

"I have no explanation, sir. Except that——" He hesitated. "I have often observed that the universe seems naturally to adapt to our beliefs and descriptions. When astronomers looked for a new planet, they found Neptune."

"It was discovered by a German. In my lifetime."

"The universe is a chameleon?" Sophia had understood the point instantly.

"So you think all of this is a figment of the imagination?" Obermann waved his arm towards the excavations. They were seated outside, close to the outlines of the stone walls.

"Not at all. But perhaps it is unknowable."

"Nonsense again. If that were so, then no progress in human understanding would ever be made."

"It is a theory."

"And one theory is as good as another?" He seemed to relent his anger. "Sophia, are you listening to Alexander?" He gave once more a peculiar emphasis to the name. "I have drawn back the curtain, and revealed the dawn. Now he tells me that it is a false dawn."

"He did not say that, Heinrich."

"My wife is defending you, Mr. Thornton. You have impressed her with your wisdom. I have solved the greatest riddle in history, and she neglects me shamefully." He put his arm around her, with an almost proprietorial air, and kissed her on the cheek.

—◦◦◦—

WHEN THE LUNCH was over Thornton walked back to the excavations with Lineau. "Do tell me more about Rawlinson," he said. "He interests me exceedingly."

"He is a tall man. Not as tall as you." Thornton wondered how Lineau could have calculated his height. "He was swift in everything he did. He had shoes that did not need lacing. He used to slip them on. He said that he did not wish to waste time in tying and untying knots. But then he might spend hours contemplating the shape of signs. He was an astonishing man." He held on to Thornton's arm. "He still lives. In a place called Cricklade. You should call on him."

"I dare not. I am in too much awe of him. To have solved the mysteries of cuneiform—"

"You are brave enough, Mr. Thornton. You dared to question Herr Obermann on his favourite theory. You dared to question Homer."

"I was merely putting forward a hypothesis."

"Herr Obermann does not deal in hypothesis or argument. This is Homer's Troy. Or it is nothing. He is a man of great conviction. He will not be withstood on these matters. If he is attacked, he is like a tiger."

"I hope I will never attack him then."

"You must make sure that you do not." Lineau seemed to look at him. "There would be a deal of fuss, as the English put it."

"We are all men of science, Monsieur Lineau. Surely we can keep our tempers."

"Ha!" If it was an expression of derision, it was uttered in the soft-est possible manner. "Herr Obermann may not agree with you on that. He is more than a man of science." He paused for a moment, and lifted his head. "Do you notice the extreme stillness of the air? It anticipates some storm."

SEVENTEEN

Later that afternoon, as Thornton was lost in his study of the clay tablets, contrasting sign with sign, he heard a low sound like a sigh coming from beneath his feet. The table at which he was working began to dance; his bed shook violently and then, as the sigh turned into a roar, the floor beneath him started to move. A pail of water rocked from side to side, and was splashed empty. His instinct was to run outside, but, first, he had to protect the tablets. Quickly, as the shaking became more violent, he gathered them together and placed them in two canvas sacks that had been used to store his soiled clothes. When he rushed outside Obermann and the others were standing by the excavations, while many of the workmen were running down the mound and on to the plain. "We are safe here!" Obermann was shouting. "Troy has endured many earthquakes!"

The trees on the mound, and on the plain, were thrashing from side to side, and the wooden roofs of two huts collapsed; the roar of the earth had gone beyond the mound and spread beneath the plain. The ground itself was rippling and swaying as if it were the sea. "Zeus is speaking!" Obermann shouted. "He is reminding us of his power!"

Thornton looked for Sophia. She was standing beside Lineau, and
had put her arm around him. She was serene amid the turmoil. Lineau's eyes were moving rapidly from side to side, but he also showed
no fear. It seemed to Thornton that Obermann was correct and that
Troy itself was somehow protected from harm. Then he watched in
astonishment as a crack opened up in the eastern part of the excavations, revealing a small chamber of stone.

The shock lasted no more than a minute, but then a dark mist of
dust, lifted upwards by a sudden draught of air, rose from the mound
and the plain. It mounted higher and higher into the air until it min-
gled with the drifting clouds.

"It is something," Obermann said, "to have heard the bellowing of
the gods who live beneath the earth. Zeus has been joined by the sons
of Tellus!" He turned to face Thornton. "So must Priam himself
have heard the voices of the unseen!" He was in a state of exaltation.
Leonid was at his side, and amid the mist of dust they looked like
identical figures.

Thornton was crying—not out of joy or pity, but because the dust
had entered his eyes. He wiped his face with the sleeve of his shirt,
and walked over to Sophia and Lineau. "Do you need any assis-
tance?" he asked them.

"On the contrary," Lineau said. "We were waiting to help you.
Sophia said that you were weeping."

"Out of discomfort, I'm afraid, not sorrow. The dust is everywhere."

"Did the trees dance?"

"Oh yes."

"That must be a fine thing to see." It was the first time that Thornton had heard him allude to his blindness.

"The ground became the waves of the sea," Sophia said. "It was
majestic. Magnificent."

"Do you see what has opened in the earth?" Thornton asked her.
"A great chasm on the eastern side."

"We cannot see it from here," she replied. "Come, Monsieur Lineau. We must look." They trod warily, as if these were their first steps on the earth, and Obermann joined them.

"We are preserved, Sophia. The gods believe in our destiny."

"Fortunate gods," Lineau said.

"If you could see the plain," Obermann told him, "you would see a prospect worthy of Mantegna. Telemachus, you must ride over to the village to see if help is needed. At once. Where is Kadri Bey?"

"He has stayed with the workmen," Leonid told him. "They fled to the bottom of the mound."

"They will be safe enough. Now, my friend Thornton, how do you find our Trojan climate?"

"Bracing."

"Bracing?" Obermann laughed. "That is a good English word. But this is much more ancient. Much darker. This is a time of omen. Of warning."

"I cannot imagine why we are being warned, sir."

"Then you must let your imagination wander further, Mr. Thornton. Have you observed that opening in the ground?"

"We were about to inspect it."

"That has been vouchsafed to us. Depend upon it. We will find something of great moment." They went carefully towards the newly opened ground, where the outline of a rectangular chamber could clearly be seen.

"There is much ash and earth to be cleared," Leonid said.

"No matter. I believe I have found what I was looking for." Obermann went over to a side wall of the chamber, beyond which a section had been cut out of rock with a flat slab upon it. "What do you believe this to be, Mr. Thornton?"

"I cannot say."

"It is a tomb. This is some ceremonial space, a room of holiness, and the tomb has been placed beside it. Quickly. While Kadri Bey remains with the workers below, we must remove the slab. I have had trouble before with the bodies of the dead. The Turks wish to bury them, against all principles of good science. If we can empty the grave before they come back, so much the better. Telemachus, go down to Kadri Bey and warn him that the excavations are not safe. Pay the men, and tell them to return next week. Kadri Bey is a coward, and will remain with them. Quickly."

"You wished me to ride to the village."

"I have changed my mind. The villagers can wait."

As Leonid ran down the slope, Obermann put his ear to the sealed rock and knocked upon the slab. "It is not hollow," he said. "There is something within it. When Telemachus returns, we must remove this covering." In the silence of the earth his voice rang out.

The mist of dust had begun to settle. Thornton feared aftershocks. Was this a false calm, about to be broken by another earthquake? For the first time he noticed thousands of birds circling in the sky, their nests disturbed or destroyed, their massed wings casting a long shadow over the mound.

Sophia looked up at the same moment. "A strange sight," she said to him. "Everything has become so strange."

"I know it. Do you notice that the birds make no noise?"

"That is the strangest thing of all."

Leonid came back. "They are returning to their villages," he said to Obermann, "to look after their families. Kadri Bey is riding to Kannakole to see what damage has been caused."

"Good. May he remain there a long time. Telemachus, we will need your strength. Are you ready, gentlemen?"

Leonid and Lineau, Obermann and Thornton tried to lift the stone slab from the enclosure of rock it had been covering. "It is too heavy," Obermann said. "We must slide it inch by inch. Sophia, will you bring me a hammer and wedge? We must split the slab from the rock."

"Surely, sir, we should record it as it lies here?"

"You have no camera, Mr. Thornton."

"I can draw."

"Then draw. Telemachus has a camera, but it will take too long to prepare it. Is that not so, Telemachus?"

"If you wish for speed."

"Immensely. I wish for it more than anything in the world."

Thornton went back to his hut. Its interior had survived the shock, but he left the canvas sacks containing the tablets outside his door. He returned with pencil and notebook, and rapidly sketched the chamber with the rock enclosure on its eastern side. Sophia had given Obermann the hammer and wedge. He began to chip away at the surface between the slab and the rock, which seemed to be no more than a compacted layer of earth. So he worked quickly and neatly, going around the sides of the slab as the dust continued to swirl about them. They were in twilight, with the massed flocks of birds obscuring the light of the sky.

"Now," he said, "we can slide the slab with ease. If Mr. Thornton has finished his drawing, he is welcome to assist us."

"Just a few moments, sir."

"It is odd, is it not, Lineau, that we are more concerned with the outward appearance than the inward reality? When you examine a vase, you raise it in your mind. You re-create it. You see with your inner eye how it once appeared to its first owner. A drawing or a photograph cannot achieve that."

Thornton had joined them, and the four men—each at one corner of the slab—managed to slide the cover away from the rock cavity. It gave way slowly, until the interior of the cavity was revealed. Within there was a small skeleton, laid out in foetal position; the bones had been stained red, and a hammerhead of some jade material had been placed beside the skull. It seemed to Sophia that Obermann was looking at it with horror rather than amazement. Thornton shook his head, and put his hands through his hair.

"What is it?" Lineau asked. "What is the consternation?"

"It is a child," Thornton said. "Its flesh has been taken from its bones, and the bones have been powdered with red ochre."

"I have seen this before." Obermann was staring at the small body. "Among the ancient tribes of Mongolia."

"It is typical of late Mesolithic burial." Thornton was eager to jump down into the small cavity, but he held back: by protocol, Obermann should enter first.

"I do not like those divisions, Mr. Thornton. I find them too imprecise. Besides, what has the Stone Age to do with this level of Troy?"

"We must take up the skeleton," Lineau said. "We cannot examine it here."

"That is not possible," Obermann replied. "It is too fragile. It may dissolve into powder and fragments. Who knows what this sudden exposure to the air will accomplish?"

"Then we must work quickly. Give me your arm, Mr. Thornton." Without waiting for Obermann's permission Lineau stepped nimbly into the cavity and, with the guidance of Thornton, knelt beside the small skeleton. In a low voice Thornton described the position and posture of the body, while Lineau ran his hands across the reddened bones. Thornton noticed an arrowhead placed beside the neck, just below the hammerhead, and whispered to Lineau.

Obermann watched them. "I am in a fever," he said, "until you speak."

"It was a boy, no more than eight or ten years of age. The bones are fine. The form is very pleasing. The norma verticalis is long and oval. The norma temporalis is extended, with a long and somewhat flat vertex curve."

"You will have to translate that, Monsieur Lineau, for the benefit of my wife."

"She will understand this. The boy was executed with an arrow shot into his neck. The arrowhead is beside him. It has been put there deliberately. And there is a break in his upper spine."

"It is not possible." Obermann's voice was very loud.

"And I will tell her something else. His flesh was eaten. There are numerous scratches on the bones that could only have been made with knives."

"Doubly impossible. Homer did not write of cannibals."

"Come and see for yourself," Thornton said.

"I do not need to see. This is not a city of death."

Sophia had been looking at the birds, which seemed to be floating above them in the sky. "It is a city of life," she said. "Life is hungry. God made it so. Life must persist."

The men had paid no attention to her, too busy in their argument over the bones. "Besides," Obermann said, "the marks could have been made by carrion birds, stripping off the flesh."

"They are too neat. Too uniform." Lineau was stroking the fibula of the child. "They occur in sequence."

"None of you has the remotest idea about archaeology. I have opened up a new world, and you wish to darken it. You want it to fall."

They all raised their heads, alerted to a change in the passage of the air. There was no noise but an abrupt and violent shaking of the earth. The men instinctively held on to one another, with Sophia joining them in terror. They formed a circle beside the small grave. The shaking lasted for only a few seconds, and then there was calm. "We have survived the after-shock," Obermann said. "Nothing more will happen."

"Look at the bones," Leonid called.

They were disintegrating in front of them, crumbling and turning to powder after their exposure to the charged air. Obermann made a sudden movement, as if to scoop them up, but the skull and part of the chest dissolved in his hands. With a cry he stepped backwards, but it seemed to Thornton to be a cry of triumph rather than of dismay.

"The bones have gone," Sophia whispered to Lineau. "They have disintegrated in the pressure of the air."

"It is not unusual. I have known swords and hammers to crumble into dust."

"It is as if they did not wish to be discovered."

"They did not wish to survive. Their work was done."

"Your cannibal theory has disappeared, Mr. Thornton." Obermann's delight was apparent to them all. "The evidence has vanished." He brushed the dust from his hands. "The will of the gods is manifest."

"I have seen it, sir."

"Your eyes can be deceived, Mr. Thornton. Did you see anything, Telemachus?" Leonid shook his head. "Sophia?"

"I had no opportunity, Heinrich."

"Nor did I." Obermann looked from one to another. "I have seen nothing. Nothing to overturn the most celebrated poem in the history of the world."

Sophia noticed Thornton's dismay and astonishment. When he walked away she followed him and touched him lightly on the shoulder. "I know that you are troubled, Alexander. I offer no excuses for my husband. He is—"

"A vandal."

"Not so harsh. He is what in Greece we call one-eyed. He sees only what he wishes."

"Like Cyclops."

"Yes. Cyclops was outwitted by Ulysses, was he not?" She hesitated for a moment. "Look for your evidence elsewhere. On the tablets. If you find it there, my husband will come round to your opinion. I am sure of it. Look for the signs."

EIGHTEEN

Three days after the earthquake Sophia noticed a black horse, with rider, slowly making its way over the plain; it seemed to be moving unsteadily but, as it drew closer, she realised that its rider was travelling side-saddle. He was dressed in black, like some appendage of the horse, and then Sophia recognised the tall stooped figure of the Reverend Decimus Harding. She associated him with the death of William Brand, and she felt uneasy. She waited for him as he tied his horse within a grove of small oak trees and climbed the mound.

"Good day to you, Frau Obermann. I trust I find you well after the shock."

"Good day to you, Father. Yes. We are all well. In good spirits."

"I am glad to hear it." He seemed strangely disappointed. "I could not rest until I had seen the damage with my own eyes."

"There is no damage, reverend sir." Obermann had come over to them. "We weathered the storm, as you say. We were strong."

"Delighted, sir. Absolutely delighted." He looked, for a moment, disconcerted. "I had heard otherwise from the English ambassador. We were all lamenting your ill fortune."

"Rumour has 'a thousand tongues,' Mr. Harding."

"As Virgil has it. I recall that you know Virgil very well." His refer- ence, to the purification of the house in the village, was very marked. "I cannot help but think the death of the American was a kind of omen."

"We do not discuss it, sir."

"Of course not. In very bad taste." Harding cleared his throat. "The ambassador believed that your excavations had been badly affected."

"Layard was mistaken." Sir Austen Layard, the English represen- tative in Constantinople, had himself once been an archaeologist who had found the palace of Sennacherib at Nineveh. "Not for the first time."

"We must not say that, Herr Obermann. Oh dear no." Harding was delighted. "Sir Austen will not thank us."

"He knew nothing of wall reliefs," Obermann said. "He did not understand the lozenge pattern."

"We must let the experts quarrel amongst themselves, dear lady. We do not understand these things." He turned to Sophia, having carefully noted the detail of Obermann's criticism. "So you have suf- fered no ill effects?"

"Troy is thriving, as you can see. Did the earthquake reach Con- stantinople?"

"The suburbs were shaken, but the old city stood firm. The Turks are not known for their composure, however. The shouting and yelling were tremendous. I thought that the end of the world had come." From Harding's expression, it seemed that he might have wel- comed that moment. "There was a slight tremor, enough to rattle the cups, but nothing more."

"Come, Reverend. Let me show you what we have uncovered." Obermann took Harding's arm, to Harding's annoyance, and guided him over the site of Troy. "The plan is simple, as you may see. The steep street here, covered with flagstones, leads from a single gate on the western side. Do you observe the foundations there?"

"This city has been in my mind's eye for many years, Herr Ober- mann. Taken from the pages of the divine Homer."

"You must not say 'divine.' Not in your profession."

"A flight of fancy, dear sir."

"I may call him the holy of holies, but for you that would be blasphemy."

"But we may call him sacred, may we not? That will not disturb the most tender conscience."

Sophia surmised that Harding's conscience was not in the least tender. "Heinrich tells me that Homer contains more beauties than the Bible. Do you agree, Father Harding?"

"It is the oldest written poem in the world, of course. It has many felicities. I am not 'Father,' dear lady, in my church. I am 'the Reverend Mr. Harding.' It is a subtle distinction."

"Now you are in the land of gods and heroes," Obermann said. "Do you see how the main street leads up to the palace here?" He beat the ground with his cane. "We have excavated many thousands of cubic metres of rubbish. I built a path to transport it. There were huge masses of debris, dear sir, sixteen metres in height!"

"I have no mind for details, Herr Obermann."

"That is why you are a priest. Do you observe this layer that descends upon these stones like black vapour? Do you perceive above it a yellow stratum of matter burned by a white heat?" Obermann was pointing his cane at some small, ruined chambers. "During the conflagration the wind must have driven the flames from the south-west, from the direction of the gate, to the north-east. All the treasures were found on the south-east side."

"Treasures, dear sir? Ahmed Nedin will be overjoyed to hear of them."

"Objects treasured by *me,* sir." Obermann spoke quickly. "Clay statuettes. Bowls."

"Nothing precious?"

"All of Troy is precious."

"But Mr. Nedin was sure that a bounty of golden ornaments would soon be handed to the museum." Decimus Harding had visited the Museum of Antiquities in Constantinople, and had met Ahmed Nedin; Nedin was an admirer of all things English, and had even spent an evening with the Reverend Mr. Harding over a hookah. "Have I told you the story of the sword?"

"Sword? What sword?" Obermann was very sharp. "I know of no sword."

"Calm yourself, dear sir. I am referring to the sword of Constantine the Twelfth."

"He was the last emperor of Byzantium. What of it?"

Sophia noticed that her husband had become unexpectedly flustered. It occurred to her that there was some skein of connections between Heinrich Obermann and Ahmed Nedin, between a promised "bounty" and the sudden appearance of the sword in the excavations. But she did not want to follow these connections. "He was defeated by Mehmet the Second, was he not?" she asked her husband.

"He was known as the Marble Emperor." Harding answered for him. "But the marble proved to be unsound."

"It proved to be the fall of Byzantium," Obermann said.

"The golden empire came to dust." Harding pronounced the phrase with relish. "The Turks conquered the glorious land. But I must tell you about the sword, Herr Obermann."

"If you wish."

"A Turkish dealer in antiquities, one known as Issed Saka—"

"I am acquainted with him," Obermann said. "A notorious lecher. A sodomite."

"He brought a sword to Ahmed Nedin, claiming it to be that of Constantine the Twelfth."

"Do not trust him."

"The museum experts confirmed that it was of Byzantine design and provenance."

"Fake. Easily achieved."

"That was precisely my reaction, dear sir. You would be surprised how many counterfeit objects arrive at the museum."

"A trained eye will discover them."

"Is that so?" Harding looked keenly at Obermann. "I must take your word for that."

Obermann seemed offended. "You may take my word for everything."

Sophia observed that her husband was growing more uneasy. "Here is Mr. Thornton," she said. "You must meet him, Reverend Mr. Harding."

Harding ignored her, and continued to address Obermann. "Several other swords, all claimed as belonging to Constantine the Twelfth, were presented to Ahmed Nedin. He has proposed a small exhibition."

"If he wishes, I will go to Constantinople and pick out the genuine."

"But you have seen him recently, have you not? When I dined with him, he extolled your virtues to me."

Obermann hesitated. "I have made a brief visit. I had no time to discuss anything of significance with him. Ah, here is a fellow Englishman for you. May I present Alexander Thornton of the British Museum?"

"Delighted. Shall we greet each other in the Turkish fashion?"

Thornton did not know what he meant. He seemed about to kiss Harding on the cheek, in response, but Harding stepped back in alarm.

"That will never do," Obermann said. "The Englishmen do not kiss each other. Not in public, at least." He put his arm around Sophia, and laughed very loudly.

——◦◦◦——

THAT EVENING, at dinner, Decimus Harding turned once more to the fall of Byzantium. "All golden things must come to dust," he said. "There is no beauty or grandeur on the earth that is not perishable."

"On the contrary," Lineau replied. "Gold survives time."

"Oh, sir, you mean mere cups and vases."

"You mistake me. I mean ideals. Aspirations. The idea of Troy has survived for thousands of years. The glory of the Byzantine Empire is still a light to the world."

"It is nonsense," Obermann said, "to compare Troy and Byzantium. They are not related."

"They may be closer than you think, Herr Obermann." Decimus Harding turned to him with a smile. "After the fall of Constantinople Sultan Mehmet the Second, the conqueror of the city, despatched a letter to the Pope. He was grieved, he said, that His Holiness was steadfast in his enmity towards him when, after all, they had common ancestors. Mehmet explained that the Teucri, the Trojans from whom the Italians were descended, belonged to the same race as the Teurci or Turks." Decimus Harding was still smiling as he spoke. "Only an accident of consonantal evolution had obscured the truth of their affinity."

"It is laughable," Obermann said. "Absurd."

Kadri Bey had been listening intently to this exchange. "Not nonsense, Herr Obermann. There are many Turks who believe that the capture of Constantinople was a just vengeance for the fall of Troy. The Greeks were at last made to pay for their perfidy. You asked me once why the Turkish villagers venerate the tombs of the Homeric heroes. Now I answer you. They are worshipping their ancestors."

"This is folly." Obermann put down his glass. "Lunacy. I cannot believe what I am hearing from you." Sophia now realised why Kadri Bey watched over the site of the excavations with such care. He believed that he was protecting his country's patrimony. "Have I not made it clear to the world? The Turks are Asiatics from the East. The Trojans were Europeans from the north."

"And where is your proof, sir?" Alexander Thornton entered the argument.

"Proof? The proof is here." He touched his head. "And here." He pointed to his heart. "I need no other guide."

"That is not evidence," Decimus Harding said, "that would stand up in a court of law."

"No jury would convict me of being an idealist. Not even in England." He had recovered his good humour. "Besides, I have a witness. Homer stands beside me. Do you really believe that Hector and the Trojan warriors are the ancestors of the Turks? I mean no disrespect to your race, Kadri Bey, but they are not the stuff of heroes."

"That is not so, Herr Obermann." Harding had intervened once again. "There is Mehmet himself, the conqueror of the Marble Emperor. There is Sultan Murad. There is Suleiman the Magnificent. All of them worthy to be celebrated by Homer himself."

"Well, I will not argue with a priest."

"The priest speaks the truth, as always." Kadri Bey did not wish to let the matter rest. "The Turks are no less valiant and determined. And they claim Troy as their own."

"We shall see," Obermann said. "The dead do not lie. They will tell us their stories. Our friend here, Mr. Thornton, will help them."

"You may not like what they tell us," Thornton said.

"In that case, I will ask them to be quiet."

NINETEEN

That same evening Heinrich Obermann organised an expedition for the amusement of his guests. "You will see, Mr. Thornton," Obermann told him, "the place where the seed of all Troy's woes was sown. Mount Ida. Surely you can spend a day or two from your scholarship to stand where Athene, Aphrodite and Hera contested for the golden apple?"

"I do not have your confidence in mythology, sir. But if you put it like that—"

"I do put it like that. There is always truth in these ancient stories. Athene appeared to Paris in shining armour and promised him supreme wisdom if he awarded the prize to her. Hera appeared in all the majesty of her royal state, and promised him wealth and power. Aphrodite approached him with the enchanted girdle around her waist, and promised him a bride as beautiful as herself. How else could he choose? Do you not crave a beautiful bride, Mr. Thornton? As beautiful as Sophia, perhaps?"

"I do not know which goddess I would choose, sir. The spur of supreme wisdom would be very strong."

"You surprise me. A young man must dream of love. Is that not so, Sophia?"

"I have no idea, Heinrich." She regretted her tone, and spoke more gently. "In matters of the heart, there can be no rules."

"There speaks a woman!" Obermann replied. "And the story proves that love is strongest. That it cannot be resisted. There is no power on earth to match it." He and Sophia glanced at one another.

"But it is the source of jealousy and division. It is the beginning of warfare." Decimus Harding had noticed the look between them. "The ancients knew that love and strife are indistinguishable."

"What do priests know of love, dear sir?"

"I see its consequences here." He looked around at ruined Troy. "Aphrodite promised Paris the most beautiful woman in the world, and so with divine aid he abducted Helen and brought her back to Troy. Of course you know the story, Frau Obermann." Harding was addressing himself to her. "Her husband, Menelaus of Sparta, enlisted Agamemnon and the other Greek lords to mount an expedition against Troy. The rest is Homer."

"You can never underestimate the force of an aggrieved husband," Obermann said. "Menelaus was implacable. His anger was unimaginable. He was willing to let many die. To allow the city to be sacked and destroyed."

"We live in more enlightened times," Harding said. "We have tamed our private passions."

"Oh have we?" Obermann turned to him. "I do not believe so."

"Would you forgive me, gentlemen?" Sophia rose from the table. "I am tired after the day's exertions."

They all rose at the same time, and Obermann was about to follow her up the slope towards their hut. "Do not forget," he said to them. "We begin at first light. We will tread in the footsteps of Paris to Mount Ida!"

———~~~———

SO JUST AFTER DAWN, on the next day, the four travellers—Obermann and Sophia, Harding and Thornton—rode slowly south-eastwards towards the mountains. They followed the track of the river Scamander as it crossed the plain of Troy. "Do you see there, gentlemen? Swans!" Obermann pointed to them excitedly. "No doubt you considered them to be English birds. The Swan of Avon. The sweet Thames."

"They are English in their bearing, don't you think?" Harding had turned to Sophia who was riding beside him. "Very stately."

She did not know if he was humouring her. "Yet they have a fierce temper," she replied. "They hiss at anyone who comes too close."

"That is only natural."

"They are beautiful in the water," Obermann observed, "but they are ugly and ungainly on land."

They rode easily across the plain, with a pack-horse carrying their supplies, past tilled fields and huts made out of mud and rushes. The sun was strong but the heat was tempered by the north-east wind that stirred the dust along the track they were following. They came to the village of Bournabashi, where they were greeted by small children who clustered around them with open hands. "Let me show you something," Obermann said. They rode off the track for a few hundred yards until they came to a hill with a stone outcrop. He pointed to it with his cane. "Johann Conze and Monsieur Chevalier both swore that this little mound was the site of Troy! Can you imagine anything more absurd and insignificant? Look. It is a place fit for beasts." Some sheep, goats and horned cattle were grazing at the foot of the hill. "My enemies are silent now, of course. They do not dare to challenge me."

"He is like the swan who hisses," Harding murmured to Thornton.

They continued their journey to Mount Ida after a brief respite, while the horses were refreshed by a spring that emerged just to the west of the outcrop of stone. The air seemed to grow clearer as they approached the mountain range, and the sound of the horses' hooves on the tracks became sharper and crisper. There were flat rocks of black basalt in the landscape around them, and when Sophia pointed them out, Thornton told her that they were the remains of lava that had once flowed down on to the plain.

"Does that mean," she asked him, "that Mount Ida was once a volcano?"

THE FALL OF TROY

"Very likely. The remains of one."

"So its life began before the gods visited it?"

"You do not need to believe these stories, Sophia."

"I do not know what to believe."

"Mythological time does not mix with geological time. They are two different worlds."

"And yet they are both part of the same world. Am I the only one who is confused?"

Thornton smiled at her. "Confusion is natural in life. We are never sure what we believe. Or what we feel."

"What we feel? Oh, I am certain of that."

"Truly?" He looked at her for a moment. "But what you feel today you may not necessarily feel tomorrow."

"Now you are confusing me again. I cannot speak to you."

"Don't say that. One of the few delights here is conversation with you."

"With me?" She seemed genuinely surprised. "But I am not clever. I am not witty."

"But you are good. You are honest. You give me hope."

"Hope for what?"

"Hope that—I don't know. Hope that everything is worthwhile. Hope for the future."

Sophia was left to ponder what that "future" might be, since Obermann now called to Thornton and pointed to the wall of a barn that they were passing. "Do you see the pieces of pottery peeping out of the clay?" he asked him. "Red and brown. They are mostly Hellenic. We must be close to the site of an ancient town, Mr. Thornton. The pottery will lie just below the surface!"

"Do you know which town it is, sir?"

"I believe it to be Scamandria. There will be a village somewhere ahead of us. There is always a settlement."

Soon enough they came upon a collection of huts, barns and dwellings. Obermann dismounted and strode into a small central store. He came out after several minutes. "This little place is called Ine," he said. "I do not know if it is a corruption of the name of the river god, Inachus, father of Io. The good woman could not tell me. But she sold me this for a trifle."

He showed them a white marble head of a woman, a beautifully polished and moulded oval that seemed to Sophia like some precious stone. She could not tell whether the face was human or divine. "Her eyes are closed," she said. "She must be sleeping."

"Sleeping or thinking," Obermann replied. "She is a good omen for our journey. She may be Athene or Aphrodite. Even with her eyes closed she will lead us forward."

They journeyed on to the town of Beiramich, which stood upon a plateau on the bank of the Scamander. Here they stopped and ate a small meal of bread and olives, as they listened to the rush of the river below them.

"Have you noticed," Sophia asked, "that the birds sing by the river but they never sing by the swamps and marshes?"

"They are imitating the sound of the water," Thornton said. "They are responding to it. There is no sound on the marshes, except that of the wind."

"Then why do the birds sing in Oxford?" Harding asked him.

"They hear the voices of the people talking. The birds are talking back to them."

"Oh, surely not? They are conversing with each other, even if we cannot understand them."

"Nobody understands anything in Oxford," Obermann said. "We must continue. It would be unwise to arrive at Ida after night has fallen."

So they rode on to the village of Evjilar. "Evjilar," Obermann said, "means village of the hunters. There are many wild beasts that come down from the mountains. Bears. Wild boars."

"Will it be safe?" Harding asked.

"Where we are going? I expect so. But you are a man of God. You will pray for us." Obermann seemed pleased by Harding's evident nervousness. "Did not Jesus tame the wild animals in the desert?"

"I do not recall that particular passage."

"You must study the Bible more closely, Reverend Harding. Besides, I have packed a pistol."

"Do you feel the air growing colder?" Sophia said.

"We are now more than eight hundred feet above sea-level," Obermann replied. "We are close to Ida."

They came next to a small clearing, with a pool of green water, while above it stretched upward the side of the mountain covered with a canopy of pine and oak and chestnut. "We will rest the horses here," Obermann said, "before we venture any further."

"And how do you propose to climb this?" Harding asked him.

"There is a track. You cannot see it from this vantage. But it has been used for thousands of years. It is the human path, dear sir. Besides, we are not ascending very far. The glade of the goddesses is below the first peak."

"I am glad to hear it."

Sophia approached Thornton as he was leading his horse towards the pool. "You have been very quiet," she said.

"Have I? I must have been distracted."

"You have been thinking of your work. It never leaves you."

"And of other things, I'm afraid." He did not look at Sophia. "The scenery here is very fine. Majestic."

"Of what other things are you afraid?"

"It is just a figure of speech. Which of these peaks is our destination, do you suppose? I must admit that I have no great experience of mountains."

"Heinrich will not test us beyond endurance. He knows the way. He has come here before. You are very secret, Alexander."

"If I cannot speak of something without embarrassment I keep silent. That is all."

Sophia sensed that her husband was coming towards them. "Alexander wishes to know our destination, Heinrich."

"We are travelling to Gargarus, Mr. Thornton, among the Ida range. That is where the goddesses descended. By great good fortune it is also the source of the Scamander. So you will see the origin. The mountain marks the beginning of the divine river. And the opening of the Trojan war. It is doubly blessed. Human beings love the start of adventures, do they not?"

They spurred on their horses, and ascended the incline of the foothill by means of a track of loose earth and stone that made its way between the thickly growing trees; then it swung around and for a mile they followed the bank of a stream that took them to a valley carving its way between two of the peaks of Ida. The floor of this valley was covered with rocks and boulders that had rolled down from the steep slopes that rose on either side. They could hear the sound of rushing water coming from somewhere above them. "You see here Mount Gargarus and Mount Cotylus," Obermann called to them, as he rode a little ahead of the main party. "The summit of Gargarus is six thousand feet above the level of the sea. Do not be concerned. We will not be climbing to the top!" He laughed. "The glade is four thousand feet below the summit of the mountain. And there we will also find the source of the Scamander. Follow me."

"I believe we have no choice," Harding muttered to no one in particular. He was not enjoying the labours of the journey.

They ascended by a narrow track, riding in single file with the pack-horse in the rear. Within an hour of hard climbing they had reached a small plateau, from which they could see the valley beneath them as well as the plain of Troy stretching out towards the sea. The only sound was that of the rushing water. "We are close to the glade of the goddesses," Obermann informed them. "But before we enter, I will show you something." They followed him on a circuitous path that seemed to go around the mountain. Then he stopped and pointed upwards. There was a natural cavern in a nearly vertical rock wall, some two hundred feet in height, and from it there issued a broad stream. It fell many feet over projecting blocks of stone until it was joined by a smaller stream and made its way as a rivulet down the side of the mountain. "The origin of the divine Scamander!" Obermann said. "It will be swollen by winter snows. It is pure! It makes the mountain fertile!" The lower slopes were indeed covered with woods, spreading over the foothills and on to the plains. "The trees here provided the timber for the ships of Paris, when he set sail to abduct Helen. Yet from this very same mountain the Greeks found the wood to build their great horse! Do you see how the land fashioned Troy's destiny? It was from here that the gods watched the battles. It was here that Aeneas was conceived by Anchises and Aphrodite. That is why I have brought you. It is part of the city."

"We will soon need wood ourselves," Harding said to Thornton, "to make a fire." He had been looking more and more anxiously at the sky. The sun was now setting, and the clear atmosphere presaged a cold night. He had not expected their journey to last so long, and did not greatly welcome a night in the Turkish countryside. Sophia, however, had been taken up by Obermann's spirit of adventure and relished every moment on the mountain. Thornton pointed out to her the waning sunlight shining upon the rock face, so that it seemed like some furnace glowing in the heart of the mountain.

"Now," Obermann said, "we may visit the three goddesses." They retraced their path a little way, then took a narrow track leading down through the rocks and gorse bushes into the trees. It was darker and more sombre here, away from the vista of the mountain range and the sound of the rushing water. The travellers were quiet. Then they came out into a small clearing, where three tall alder trees rose close together. "Holy ground," Obermann said.

They dismounted and tethered their horses to oak trees on the periphery of the clearing. "The trees grow where the goddesses once stood. The alder tree loves water. They love the Scamander, as the goddesses did."

To Harding's amazement, Obermann then went down upon his knees and bent his head in prayer. The clergyman did not feel that he could countenance this act of worship, so he walked to the edge of the clearing and looked among the trees. Then he took a sudden step backwards. He thought that he had seen something moving in the foliage. He rejoined the others very quickly, just as Obermann was rising to his feet. "We may set up our camp here," Obermann said. "While there is still light we must collect fallen branches for a fire." He laughed at Harding's expression of dismay. "We have all packed food in our saddle-bags, and I took the precaution of bringing four blankets. The ground here is very smooth."

They collected firewood easily enough from the forest just beyond the glade, and placed it in a large pile away from the three alder trees. As the sky darkened, a full moon was visible above the mountains. It seemed close to the earth here, the silver orb striated with the marks of its own valleys and mountains. "I know what we must do," Obermann said.

"I do hope," Harding muttered to Thornton, "that it is not some kind of ceremony. He is very pagan, don't you think?"

"I think that is his way of maintaining good relations."

"Relations? With whom?"

"The Trojans. The land."

Obermann had gone over to the pack-horse and taken from one of its satchels the marble head he had purchased in Ine. "This is the prize," he said. "Sophia, you must choose between us and award it to the most deserving."

"You are copying the legend, Herr Obermann," Harding said. "Is that wise? What if we were to start another conflict?"

"What conflict could there possibly be? We are not divine beings. Mr. Thornton will not abduct anyone. At least I hope he will not."

"I do not know what I am supposed to do, Heinrich."

"Here. We will line up before you. Mr. Harding is the most devout. I am the most adventurous. Mr. Thornton—well, he is the most handsome. You must simply choose between us." They stood just in front of the three alder trees, and the clear moon made them seem for a moment like figures of marble, silent and motionless in the silver light. The sculptured head lay on the ground between them and Sophia.

"I cannot do it, Heinrich."

"How can she judge between us, sir?" Thornton asked him.

"A woman always knows."

"I am not so sure of that," Harding said. "You may remember Eve."

And then they heard the howling of a wolf, somewhere close to them. The horses whinnied and became restless, while Obermann walked to the edge of the clearing and peered into the darkness of the surrounding trees. "It is a warning," he said, when he returned to the others. "Nothing more."

"You are being told," Sophia said, "not to imitate the gods."

"It is possible."

"I thought I saw something move between the trees." Harding was clearly nervous.

"At the time of the full moon," Obermann said, "a wolf may possess a human soul. As a child in Germany, I was taught that. Yet whose soul would wish to be with us tonight?" He looked at Sophia. She had, for an instant, thought of William Brand.

While they were talking, Alexander Thornton had been gathering up more branches from the glade and the forest beyond it. He brought them into the centre of the clearing, and placed them on the pile. "A fire will keep any animals at bay," he said. He took a box of Lucifer matches from one of his pockets, and soon enough there was a blaze that spread warmth and glimmering light around the glade.

"We will sing," Obermann said. "We will sing loudly. That will keep off the beasts of the night. I will sing to you 'Einerlei' and then 'Meinem Kinde'!" He sang boisterously, and then recited another ballad that began "Für fünfzehn pfennige." The others had not understood a word, but when Thornton took the lead with a version of "The Sobbing Deer" and "Where the Bee Sucks," Decimus Harding joined the chorus. They continued singing until they were too tired to think of any more songs, and then all of them slipped quietly into sleep as the fire sank down. In the forest, there was no noise.

—✺—

THE NEXT MORNING they were in good spirits, relieved and pleased that there had been no incursion in the night. Any danger had safely passed. But as they packed away the blankets and levelled the charred remnants of the fire, Obermann called, "It has gone!" He put his hands on his hips and stood perplexed. "It has been taken!"

"What are you talking about, Heinrich?"

"I left it here on the ground." The sculpture—the marble head—was missing.

"It must be there," Harding said. "How could it have disappeared?"

They looked throughout the glade, in case the marble had rolled away by some strange motion. They looked in the forest immediately beside the glade. "What is the explanation for this?" Obermann asked them, as if he were challenging them.

"A wild bear may have taken it in the night," Thornton said, smiling. "They may collect such things."

"And made no noise to wake us," Obermann replied. "I hardly think so."

"Could one of us have walked in our sleep?" Harding was also smiling. "But we would scarcely have walked into the forest."

"What is your explanation?" Sophia asked Obermann.

"I do not know." He looked at the others carefully. "You will laugh at me if I propose some divine agency—"

"The three goddesses came down and removed a rival. Is that it?"

"Not so fast, reverend sir. Do not forget that this is a sacred place. That may be why the wolves did not touch us."

"So," Sophia said, "the marble was their reward for protecting us."

"Oh, really," Harding said.

"It could be so." Obermann put his arm around his wife. "Sophia has a female understanding of these deities. They may have wished for a gift."

TWENTY

Over the next few weeks, after Decimus Harding's return to Constantinople, Sophia became more interested in Thornton's meticulous study of the clay tablets; she came into his hut and, sitting side by side, they would pore over the signs and symbols that he placed on the wooden table. She was also able to draw them with great precision, and they would compare each other's interpretations of the shapes they saw. What for Thornton seemed to be a bundle of arrows was, for Sophia, a sheaf of wheat.

In turn Thornton began to question her about her own awakened interest in the small votive figures that were regularly found in the ground of Troy. Some were of terracotta, and were perfectly formed with the heads of men and women; others were much more crudely fashioned, but there were still clues to their meaning. Sophia had noticed inscribed lines on the backs of some, for example, which seemed to represent the long hair of a female goddess. "What is peculiar," she said to him, one morning, as she showed him a crude idol of bone, "is that some of the other figures are so carefully sculpted. It is as if a living artist had created them." They were standing together, in the hut where she and Obermann lived, just above the cavity in the floor where the treasures were concealed.

"What do you make of this?" He pointed to four horizontal lines below the head.

"That is her armour. The two breasts are below. And the crossed lines upon the body also give her a warlike appearance."

"And this?"

"Her vulva, I believe."

"Our friends were lacking in delicacy."

"They were not afraid of life. This is the source of the world, Alexander."

" 'Bliss was it in that dawn to be alive.' " He seemed confused for a moment. "I'm sorry. I am only quoting."

"There is nothing to be sorry for. It is a wonderful sentiment. When the sons and daughters of Eve came into the world, there must have been great joy. Here is another goddess with the same mark. Do you see?"

"The Trojans had a much more healthy notion of their gods. They could enjoy—"

"Intercourse between the sexes? Oh, yes. That was part of their divinity. That is what we have in common with them."

"I believed you to be a Christian, Sophia."

"Not here. Christianity has nothing to do with Troy." She put the figurine up to the light. "She was a goddess of life. The equivalent of Rhea. Now do you see this? It is a figurine made into a child's toy, I believe. Or it may have been a lucky charm carried in clothing. Do you see? Instead of the face there is a carved circle."

"I do not think that it was meant for a child. It is too fierce."

"I would not say that it was fierce. It is an ancient image. That is all."

"And what is this?" He picked up a heavy object of diorite, which had five projections or globes.

"Do you notice these faint incised lines? That is the necklace. So that globe is the head." She stood it upright. "The arms and the legs are in place," she said. "It is too strange. It still possesses a spirit."

He stepped back. "This might have been owned by the child."

"The one whose body we found? His spirit has fled, I am afraid."

"Is that what gave the child life in the first place? A spirit?"

"Of course," she replied.

"I used to call it the soul."

"Oh the soul is too inert. It dwells within you like some stone. But the spirit leaps and dances. It is the sap in the tree, the blood in the veins."

"I never know when you are being serious, Sophia."

"Oh, I am never serious."

"I have seen you silent. Then you are serious enough. When you look across the plain towards the Hellespont and curl your hair in your hands."

"You have been watching me! That is unfair."

"I often watch you."

"Do not do it. I am now being serious, Alexander. Please do not do it."

Her consternation made it clear to him that he had gone too far. He looked around, not wishing to meet her gaze, and noticed that her cloak and hat had been dropped casually upon the bed. Obermann's packet of American cigarettes was on a side-table. "You are comfortable here, Sophia."

"Comfortable? I would hardly call it that." She laughed. "I manage, as my husband says."

"Yet you enjoy your work on these."

"They are my life now." She was silent for a moment. She already relented the annoyance she had shown to him. "I have never admitted that to anyone before."

"I admire you, Sophia." He correctly interpreted her glance. "I cannot speak. I, too, will be silent."

———

WHEN HE WENT BACK to his hut he took out a letter that he had begun writing to the head of the department of Proto-historical Scripts at the British Museum. Alfred Grimes was a friend as well as a colleague, and Thornton felt impelled to describe to him the finding and sudden destruction of the small skeleton after the earthquake.

It would be a means of placing it on record, albeit in unofficial form, and thus of preserving some vestige of the real conditions of Troy.

"My dear Grimes," he had written, "I am here on the summit of the fortress hill of Hissarlik, otherwise known as Troy. It is in many respects a glorious place—nowhere else in the world has the earth revealed so many remains of ancient settlements lying upon one another, with such rich contents within them." He then went on to describe the layers of the various settlements of Troy, and in particular explained the discovery of the "Burned City" of which Homer was deemed to have written. On another page he expressed his delight at the opportunity of studying the clay tablets. "I do believe that they are some of the first evidences of writing in the world," he told Grimes. "It is possible that they existed prior to the scripts of Mesopotamia, but on this, as on so many other matters, I can reach no firm conclusion as yet." He described his faltering progress in deciphering the symbols but affirmed his belief that in the end "I will find my way through all the thickets."

He stopped for a moment, and then began another paragraph.

You know Herr Obermann by reputation as a somewhat aggressive and overbearing fellow. That reputation is fully justified. He is a real Teuton. He regards archaeology as a tool for his theories, and has absolutely no regard for evidence. He orders the destruction of anything Roman or Greek so that he can uncover the prehistoric. Whenever potsherds of classical antiquity are uncovered, he treats them with disgust. If in the course of the work they fall into his hands, he throws them away! He looks with displeasure at each stirrup jar that emerges from the earth. And there has been one troubling and rather unpleasant incident.

Then in rapid handwriting Thornton sketched the discovery of the child's powdered skeleton.

I saw and felt the unmistakable marks of a knife applied to the bones, and of the flesh being scraped from the bones, but Herr Obermann pro-

fessed the sublimest indifference to the matter, and positively rejoiced when the poor child's skeleton began to disintegrate after its unwelcome exposure to the air. He refused to believe that his blessed Trojans were engaged in ritual sacrifice or ritual cannibalism, despite the fact that it is well attested in the ceremonies of other primitive tribes. As far as he is concerned, his Trojans are not primitive at all. They are Homeric heroes in gorgeous armour.

Thornton stopped again, and reflected on his words. "So I ask you to keep this letter safe until my return, when I fully intend to publish the details of the incident. I am enclosing a drawing I made of the site of the burial." He followed this with his good wishes to his other colleagues at the British Museum, and signed, "Cordially yours, A. Thornton." Then he placed the paper in a envelope, and sealed it.

The following morning he gave the letter to a Turkish boy, Rashid, whose duty it was to run errands between Hissarlik and Kannakale.

———

OBERMANN HAD BEEN walking towards the "armoury" where the finds were stored; ever since the sword had been discovered, he had given the hut that name. He had glimpsed Thornton giving a small packet to the boy, and waited in the doorway until Thornton had gone. Then he called him over. "Rashid, what have you there?" He glanced at the inscription on the envelope. "I am riding to Kannakale this morning. I will take it." He gave the boy his customary tip. "Do not tell Mr. Thornton," he said. "He will ask you to return his piastre."

He went back to his quarters, since he knew that Sophia was busy in a trench where some jade beads had been discovered. He removed the letter from its envelope and, whistling softly, he read it very quickly. "The Englishman is upset with me," he said to himself. "I am not a good sport." Then he lit a candle, and burned the letter.

———

SOPHIA NOTICED that her husband was very jovial that evening, over dinner. He was particularly attentive to Thornton, insisting that he have a second helping of canned peaches, which he had mixed with some curaçao he had brought to the table in his hip-flask. "It is not ambrosia," he said, "but we are not gods. We are mortal men. We must eat canned peaches. Are they to your taste, Mr. Thornton?"

"We are not heroes, either," Lineau said. He did not care for canned fruit.

"What was that, my friend?"

"The age of heroes is past."

"Ah, Lineau, you are a pessimist. Is that your belief also, Mr. Thornton? Has the age of heroes passed away?"

"I could not say."

"Surely you have an opinion on the matter? Your friend, Rawlinson, for example. Will he be remembered in a thousand years' time?"

"He is not my friend, but I esteem him very highly."

"So he is a hero, then?"

"I don't know if the word has any weight. It has changed since the days of Troy."

"I challenge you, Mr. Thornton."

"I beg your pardon?"

"I challenge you to race with me three times around the circuit of Troy. Just as Hector and Achilles did. They ran three times around the city in heroic contest. Shall we be heroes? Shall we follow their steps?"

"It was not a contest," Lineau said. "It was a pursuit to the death."

"But we are sportsmen. We are more enlightened than the savage Trojans, are we not, Mr. Thornton?"

"I have reason to think so, sir."

"Then we will simply race on the plain. Will you be Achilles fleet of foot or Hector of the flashing helmet?"

Thornton laughed. "Achilles is too terrible. I had rather share the fate of Hector."

"So be it. You have spoken. Tomorrow we will run where Homer has described. They began before the great gates of Troy, just beneath the wall. They passed the watch-tower and the wild fig tree before they came upon a wagon track and the two fair flowing fountains that feed the Scamander. They passed the washing tanks, where we have found the stone cisterns. That is our course."

"But what is to be the prize?" Sophia asked him.

"Immortal glory."

"Do not let history repeat itself," Kadri Bey whispered to Thornton. "Hector was killed by Achilles, and his body was dragged across the dusty plain."

"I know it. I do not think Herr Obermann dislikes my theories to that extent."

"In running around the city three times," Obermann was saying, "we will cover almost ten miles. Is that daunting, Mr. Thornton?"

"Not at all."

"In your public school you will have run greater distances."

"But not through such grand terrain. Sussex has no mountains."

"You were educated in the land of the south Saxons? It accounts for the sturdiness of your beliefs. I admire the Saxon mind. It is so practical."

"They believed in justice, certainly."

"As do we all. In justice, as Hector, you are allowed to begin the race. I give you thirty seconds." Then Obermann rose from the table, and took Sophia by the arm; they walked back slowly, and Obermann could be heard interpreting a part of the night sky to his wife.

TWENTY-ONE

On the following morning, much to the surprise of the Turkish workers, Obermann and Thornton stood in shorts and linen shirts before the stone blocks that marked the original gateway of Troy. Sophia, Lineau and Leonid were with them, and Leonid handed each of them a metal cup of water from the spring. It seemed to be an unequal contest—Obermann was a heavy-set man, with the ordinary stoutness of middle age, while Thornton was young enough still to have retained his slender and muscular physique.

"Sophia," Obermann said, "you will be good enough to strike this for the commencement." He presented to her a large bronze bowl, with incised rim, that had been unearthed from one of the storerooms of the ancient palace. "Telemachus, you will go ahead of us and supervise the course. You will observe our progress, like the gods who watched the flight of Hector. You have the start of thirty seconds, Mr. Thornton."

Sophia was astonished at her husband's confidence. How could he possibly compete with this athletic young man in a race of ten miles? He was already perspiring in the morning sun. Yet he seemed eager and determined. Leonid walked up, with a leather satchel holding a container of water.

"You will be the fawn, Mr. Thornton, and I will be the hound. Once you have started from the covert, on this bright morning, I will track you through the glades and groves."

"Homer?"

"He inspires me with great energy. Do you remember that passage on the dream, where a man cannot overtake the one who runs before him? We will see if that dream comes true. Are you ready, Sophia?"

Sophia took up the bronze bowl, and struck it with the flat of her hand; on that dull thud Thornton began to run around the course. Obermann watched him and in a loud voice counted thirty seconds. Then after blowing a kiss to his wife he sprang off after him. He seemed to Sophia to be immensely light-hearted, and in fact he ran much more quickly than she had expected; he had a way of carrying his bulk gracefully, so that he cut neatly through the air. But there was no possibility that he could catch Thornton, who had the speed and concentration of a practised runner. The two men disappeared from sight.

"What is the point of this?" she asked Lineau, who was standing to one side of her.

"Your husband wants to teach the Englishman a lesson. I do not yet know what it is."

"By losing to him? Surely that is what will happen."

"It might be that, on being victorious over a much older man, Thornton will learn something. It is possible. The ways of your husband are sometimes mysterious."

Eventually Thornton came back into sight, running at a slightly more measured pace but with no sign of discomfort. He waved at Sophia, but said nothing. Two or three minutes later Obermann appeared; he had acquired a steady, relatively fast, pace that seemed to suit him. "I am fit!" he called to Sophia. "My daily swim has toughened me! I am an eagle darting through the clouds to the plain!"

"If the race were twenty circuits," Lineau said, "Herr Obermann might win. I sense his persistence."

"I am beginning to understand him," she said. "He will win at all costs."

"Unless there is a bolt of lightning, that will be difficult."

"It would not surprise me, Monsieur Lineau, if my husband could summon lightning."

"Do you believe him to be dangerous?" Lineau's tone was light and playful. "Surely not?"

"Oh, no." Sophia was equally playful. "But his gods are dangerous."

"And if he could invoke them—"

"Fortunately, that is no longer possible."

"A mortal man, then?"

"But he takes mortality to its limits, don't you think?"

"He attempts to do so, Frau Obermann." Lineau was silent for a moment. "I envy you."

"Whatever for?"

"You will live long enough to see if he succeeds or not."

Thornton now came back into view on the second circuit of the old city. He seemed as fresh and as energetic as before. Sophia was about to talk to him, but he put up his hand. "I am perspiring too freely," he said. "I am not fit for human company."

Four minutes after he had receded into the distance Obermann appeared, keeping up the same pace and momentum that he had acquired at the beginning. He called out a line of Greek to Sophia as he passed her, but she did not catch the words.

"Aesop," Lineau said. "The hare and the tortoise."

On the third circuit, to Sophia's astonishment, Obermann emerged alone. She called to him, even while he was still in the distance. "Where is Alexander?"

Obermann seemed to shrug his shoulders, but he did not reply until he came close to her. "Hector is sprawled in the dust."

"Why? What has happened?"

"I did not wait to discover." Obermann laughed, but did not vary his stride until he had reached the stone blocks where the race ended. "Achilles has triumphed!" He walked over to Sophia, his arms outstretched. "Where is the wreath for the victor? Do you not wish to congratulate your glorious husband?"

"I must go to him." She disengaged herself from his embrace. "He may be injured."

"Telemachus will attend to him. Look. They are approaching. The hare is limping, but he is unharmed."

Sophia could see Thornton being supported by Leonid, as they made their way slowly towards them. She was surprised by the keen concern that she felt for him; she looked on anxiously as he seemed to sway against Leonid. When they drew closer she noticed how pale he seemed.

"What is the matter?" she asked him.

"Ankle." He tried to smile but could manage only a grimace.

"Did you fall?"

"Something hit me on the back. A stone. A rock. I felt the pain and fell forward. Then I stumbled."

"It is not broken," Obermann said. "It is sprained. Let Mr. Thornton rest against you, Telemachus. We will carry him back."

"A rock?" Sophia was incredulous.

"It is not possible." Obermann answered her question. "There was no one near you, Mr. Thornton. Did you see anyone, Telemachus?" Leonid shook his head. "They could not have thrown a missile at you from the walls of Troy. You slipped and fell. That is all."

"I felt it. It threw me off balance."

"Then this is a mystery, Mr. Thornton."

"It could have been a stone fallen from the beak of a bird," Leonid ventured. "Such things have happened."

"In that event," Obermann said, "it would have been an omen. But I do not think that Mr. Thornton believes in omens."

"It must have left a mark upon my back."

Obermann investigated Thornton's skin. "There is no mark here. Not even a scratch. It is my belief that you were hit by an arrow from Athene. The arrows of the gods are invisible."

"And why should Athene wish to strike him?" Lineau asked.

"She wishes to preserve the honour of the founder of Troy!"

"Not the founder, surely?"

"Finder, not founder." Obermann laughed. "I have mistaken the words."

"It was a stone." Thornton was very clear. "It was hurled at me with great force."

"But it left no bruise."

"If it had hit my head, I could have been killed."

"But you were not killed!" Obermann clapped his hands. "You have only sprained your ankle. If you were not an Englishman, I might accuse you of being a bad loser."

TWENTY-TWO

Thornton's injured ankle gave him the opportunity to remain within his quarters, where he continued to study the clay tablets intently. If he gazed at the signs for long, they became formless, a wilderness of lines and marks, so he carefully divided his time and attention between different aspects of the decipherment. He compared the tablets with various Egyptian hieroglyphics, for example, looking for resemblances; he studied the rows of symbols for any evidence of association with the cuneiform of Mesopotamia. He separated the signs that were clearly pictures or ideograms from those he considered to be phonetic in character; of the phonetic groups, he believed that he could distinguish eight different units or syllables. "These are records of some kind," he told Sophia one afternoon. She came each day to examine his ankle, and to anoint it with bear's grease that she had purchased in Kannakale; it was supposed to be a sovereign cure for muscular strain, and indeed Thornton's ankle was now greatly improved. "And, since they are records, they are brief and to the point. They are placed in units."

"If they are records," she said, "they will contain numbers."

"Precisely so. Do you see these signs at the end of each row?"

"And what are these marks at the beginning of the lines? They resemble each other."

"Well observed. I do not yet know what they represent. My guess is that they signify a change of tense, or a different case ending. Plural rather than singular. Accusative rather than nominative. If they are evidence of grammatical inflection, then—I am sorry, Sophia. I am boring you with my nonsense."

"It is not nonsense at all. It is pure sense. It is sense from the beginning of the world."

"So many tablets are burned or decayed. Sometimes I feel as if I am searching among ashes."

"My husband has taught me to value the evidence of fire. So much is preserved by it."

"When fire breaks out—"

"Yes?" She suddenly became wary.

"Who can tell what will be saved and what lost? Do you see? This appears to me to be a clay label, but the object to which it was attached has been destroyed. Here is a clay seal, but I cannot make out the symbol. Is it a dancing figure? Or is it a heron?"

"You will have to be patient, Alexander."

"I know it. Troy was not built in a day. May I ask you a question, Sophia?"

"If it is a reasonable one."

"Are you happy in this place?"

"I am content with it. I am busy with the work we do."

"You have no regrets about coming here?"

"You are asking me if I have any regrets about my marriage."

"Oh no. Nothing of the kind." He was clearly embarrassed. "I would never ask such a question."

"And I would never answer it. Are *you* happy here?"

"I am happy with my work, like you. It is the most fascinating I have ever done. It is overwhelming." They examined two or three tablets in silence, but then Thornton laid them down. "There is something else I must ask you, Sophia."

"What is it?" She seemed alarmed, and put her hand up to her throat.

"Do you not notice—do you not feel—a certain strangeness here?"

"What do you mean?"

"I was hit by a stone that vanished. The bones of that child disappeared in front of us."

"That was simple exposure to the air. It is quite common."

"Not just that. Everything. The earthquake, too. You must have noticed other things."

"Nothing out of the ordinary." She did not mention the sudden death of the American, William Brand, because she did not know how to describe it. Instead she had a vivid recollection of something else; she heard once more the cry of the woman on the farm of Theodore Skopelos. "You are in unfamiliar surroundings. That is all."

"Quite. I am being fanciful. You do not approve."

"You do not need my approval, Alexander."

"On the contrary. I feel that I need your support."

"To do what?"

"To stay here."

She leaned forward, and kissed him lightly on the cheek. "There. I am supporting you, Alexander."

—◆◆◆—

LATER THAT AFTERNOON Kadri Bey, in high excitement, brought to Thornton a number of tablets that had been found undisturbed in one of the most recent excavations of a "kitchen" or "eating area" in which had already been found the bones of goats, sheep and aurochs. "I am happy to present these to you, Mr. Thornton," he said. "If I may hazard my own poor opinion, they are considerably older than the others. They have been found at much greater depth."

"How were they stored?"

"In a stone oven. I wish you joy."

On examining them later that day, Thornton found that Kadri Bey's speculation had been correct. These were all pictures or picture-words, ideograms, much like the earliest known hieroglyphics. There was the image of a fish, and of a palm tree; there seemed to be a boat, and a mountain. On studying these images Thornton believed that he was looking into a lost world in which every natural thing was sacred and charged with life. Another tablet intrigued him. It showed four horizontal lines, with four circles in a row above them; to the right-hand side was the image of a hammer or an axe. Inside each circle were two dots or points. If Thornton had been a mathematician, he might have puzzled over this equation for some time. But he realised, with an intake of breath, that the circles were heads. The four heads were detached from the four bodies lying horizontally beneath them; they had been cut by the axe that completed the ideogram. It was a record of four killings or sacrifices. "I know it now," he whispered to himself. "This was a city of death."

TWENTY-THREE

The recollection of the woman's cry had stayed with Sophia, even after she had left Thornton's quarters and returned to her own. For her that cry was associated with the sternness of Maria Skopelos, with the sight of the goat dancing to the music of the flute and, curiously enough, with the sudden arrival of Leonid after her long sleep. There was no obvious connection between these matters, but for Sophia they seemed to form a pattern for which she could not find the thread. Why had she fainted, or fallen asleep, in the company of Maria and Theodore? Leonid had arrived with the purpose of escorting her back. And this was the odd thing. He had not reacted to the cry of the woman. He had insisted that the goat, excited after its dance, had made Maria shriek out loud in the kitchen. But she was sure that it had been a cry of anguish. So she determined upon a journey.

"I am riding into Kannakale," she told her husband, on the following morning. "I have a longing to see shops and markets."

"A woman speaks! You have every right to buy nice things, Sophia. You deserve the finest. Frau Obermann must be perfect."

"Do you think the Central Hotel will be suitable?"

"You wish to stay there? Of course. They know me well. I will ask Telemachus to go ahead and reserve the largest suite for you."

"No, Heinrich. This is my adventure. I will arrange everything."

"Whatever you desire. Buy silk and linen. Buy fine shoes. Here is gold for you." He went over to a corner of their quarters, and took some coins from a vase.

"No, Heinrich. I have money of my own. And I have my jewels from Athens. I do not need gold."

"As you wish." He seemed disappointed. "You will be Artemis disguised as a mortal woman, stepping in a bright cloud among the people."

"I hardly think so. We are all mortal."

"Never say it, Sophia. We are gods in our ambitions. The will is god."

"I have a dangerous husband."

"A loyal husband. A faithful husband who offers you gold." He laughed. "There is no woman on earth who could resist me."

"We will not put the matter to the test. Now I must prepare."

She had conceived no definite plan. She was not even sure of her intention, other than to ride out to the farm and discover more about Maria and Theodore Skopelos. She realised, of course, that she would then find out more about her husband's previous life. So, as she rode on the dusty track towards Kannakale, she was excited by a vague sense of trespass and of guilt. Two kites sailed above her, and seemed to be watching her, so she spurred on the horse and rode faster; the birds continued their languid course above the plain, and she smiled at her own folly.

When she reached the town she decided to stop at the Central Hotel and reserve a room; if her visit to the farm proved fruitless, she would need somewhere to sleep that night. While the horse was being fed and watered in the courtyard, she lay upon her bed as the wooden fan revolved slowly above her. And then she noticed that she was trembling. It was not the coolness of the room after the heat of the journey. It was fear. Of what should she feel afraid? Or was it some general terror that had afflicted her? She stood up and walked over to the window, from where she could see the people of Kan-

nakale engaged in the usual activity of the town. And slowly the fear
left her.

———✺———

SHE TOOK THE ROAD out of Kannakale, which wound along the
coast towards the village of Karamic. It was already afternoon, and
the heat of the day bore heavily upon her; she had eaten and drunk
nothing since her departure from Hissarlik. There was a stream somewhere close to her, but she did not trust the brackish and slow-mov-
ing water of the plain. When she saw the stone hut of the watcher of
the sea, however, she forgot her weariness. She hesitated to disturb the
hermit in his meditation, but she knew that it was customary to offer
refreshment to the passing traveller. When she approached the small
dwelling, she saw that the door was open.

She tethered her horse to the wooden post by the side of the hut,
and walked towards the open door. He had sensed her presence before he had heard her footsteps, and asked in Turkish who was there.
She had learned a few words from the workers in Hissarlik, and was
able to explain in his own language that she was a traveller in need of
water. He came on to the threshold. He was very tall, and pale, his
long dark hair about his shoulders; he had a moustache and a beard,
also grown long. He did not look at her; he kept his eyes averted, out
of politeness or humility. He told her that there was water for her,
plentiful water, but that she must remain outside. He went back into
the hut and returned with a pitcher and bowl. Still he did not look at
her. It was perhaps not permissible for him to look at a woman. She
drank greedily from the proffered bowl, and he seemed to clench and
unclench his hands as she did so. As soon as she had thanked him, he
looked at her. It was as if she had suddenly been shaken by some material force. His eyes were so pale that the irises seemed almost white,
the palest blue against snow. There was nothing there but silence and
solitude and mourning; in the pale eyes of the hermit, she saw caves
and barren mountains and lonely paths. Then he looked away, and
the sensation was gone.

He asked her where she was going, and she pointed in the direction of the farm. He shook his head. "Do not go there," he told her. "A mad woman lives there. Mad woman!" *Deli kadin!* As he repeated the phrase, he held out his arms and looked down at the ground as if he were some image of crucifixion.

She thanked him for the gift of water, and left him. It was as she had suspected. The strange cry had come from a woman whom the watcher of the sea deemed to be mad. Had he observed her along the small paths and trackways of this neighbourhood? Or, more likely, had he heard reports from those who left him offerings of food and drink? She rode more slowly now, reflecting upon the connection between her husband and Theodore Skopelos. She turned a bend as the path followed the track of the stream, and was alerted by a sudden sound—a little way ahead of her was the unmistakable figure of Leonid riding upon his white horse towards the farm. She dismounted immediately, and waited in the shade of an alder tree growing beside the stream. Why had Leonid returned? Had he come to retrieve the treasures that she had carried here so many weeks before? It seemed the most likely explanation. Nevertheless, she was curious. She left her horse tethered by the stream, and set off along the dirt path.

She could see the farm buildings ahead of her, and she slowed her pace. She did not wish to come too close. She did not yet want to be seen. Then she heard the laughter—hysterical laughter, wild laughter filled with misery. It was the laughter of the mad woman. Sophia could not help walking forward. It was as if she were drawn towards this despair. Then she could see the figures in the yard; on going closer, she could make out the profile of Leonid. He was sitting on the ground, while beside him stood a woman wrapped in a white sheet or blanket. Her grey hair hung down to her shoulders, and her face was savage; it looked as if it had been moulded, eaten away, by monstrous thoughts. Then the woman dropped to her knees and the two of them—Leonid and the woman—began to paw each other like dogs in a dog game. Sophia could not endure this. She continued walking forward, more quickly now. The woman sensed her first, and growled at her.

Leonid turned, and saw Sophia coming towards him. He rose to his feet.

"What is this terrible thing, Leonid? What are you doing here?" He shook his head and said nothing. He looked at her as if he pitied her. "Answer me. What are you doing?"

"Sophia, this is my mother."

The woman shrieked at Sophia, crying out in Russian, "Mother! Mother!" *Matrishka!*

Sophia stood quite still. And then she understood. She turned and fled, running as fast as she could while pursued by the laughter of the woman. She did not stop until she had reached her horse. She mounted it hastily, and galloped away.

TWENTY-FOUR

On the morning of Sophia's departure Thornton had woken earlier than usual; immediately he opened his eyes, he knew that he had solved one of the riddles posed by the tablets. The language was not Greek at all and had no relation to Greek. He knew its origin.

He came out of his quarters just as Obermann was embracing Sophia before she rode to Kannakale. Thornton looked away. He took no pleasure in the spectacle of Obermann kissing his wife.

"You rise early, Mr. Thornton," Obermann said to him, as he walked back to the excavations. "You will catch the worm."

"I have much to do."

"The tablets are exercising you? What are your thoughts on the subject? May I?" He did not wait for an answer, but walked into Thornton's hut. He saw the tablets lying upon the table, and picked one up. He seemed to be examining it carefully. "Homer said that there was a language of men and a language of gods. Perhaps this is the language of the gods."

"I hardly think so, Herr Obermann. This is certainly the language of men." Thornton could scarcely conceal his eagerness and excitement. "But they are not the men you imagine."

"Oh?" Obermann was very casual.

"Let me show you something. Do you see this sequence of signs? They meant nothing to me at first, but then I identified seven separate variants."

"Seven separate case forms?"

"Precisely. What does that mean to you?"

"I am a man of earth and stone, Mr. Thornton. I cannot follow your speculations."

"They are identical with ancient Sanskrit. And do you see this? These two separate signs are placed at the ends of many words. I believe them to signify tenses. I have interpreted them as *ya* and *tva*. Do you know what they are, Herr Obermann?"

"You will tell me."

"Ancient Sanskrit." Obermann looked at him impassively. "Do you not see? The Trojans spoke the language of the ancient Vedas. They are the people of the Rigveda and the Samaveda!"

"Impossible, sir. Preposterous. They were Greek, not Indian."

"I did not say that they were Indian. They were part of the people who had their origin in Punjab and Uttar Pradesh. They were infinitely more ancient than the Greeks. Does that not excite you?" Obermann remained silent. "This is evidence of writing long before the introduction of the Phoenician or the Greek alphabets. It is a revelation!"

"You have made a mistake in your interpretation, Mr. Thornton. It is not true. It is a false impression."

"Upon what evidence, sir, do you base that opinion?"

"It is not my opinion. It is my judgement."

"But your judgement, as you call it, must be informed."

"Informed? I have spent my life and my fortune studying this city, Mr. Thornton."

"That is not to the point."

"I have laboured night and day to open up a new world for archaeology. I have done what nobody else has ever done or could ever do."

"You speak only of yourself—"

"Do not interrupt me. Troy will now stand as long as this globe is inhabited by men. The people of Troy have been celebrated by Homer and a thousand other poets from the first moment that poets ever sang. They have always been European, not Asiatic. The idea that they came from the east is preposterous. Are we to overthrow the universal tradition for the sake of your theory?"

Thornton, despite his attempt to remain calm, had become very angry. "Let me show you this, Herr Obermann. Tell me if this is my theory." He picked up the clay tablet that displayed the axe and the four severed heads. "Do you see the victims and the means of their death? This is an image of human sacrifice!"

Obermann turned away his head. He would not look at it. "Do you think that I am interested in this nonsense?" He snatched the tablet from Thornton and threw it into a corner. "You have decided to destroy me and my work. You have been set upon me by my enemies in England, who will never rest until I am ridiculed and silenced."

"I have no such intention." As soon as Obermann shouted at him, Thornton regained his composure. "I am telling you what I have discovered. That is all."

"What *you* have discovered? And what of *my* discoveries? I have performed miracles, Mr. Thornton. No one in England understands that. Your little museum is a nest of adders waiting to strike at me."

"Believe me, sir, that is not true. We venerate your name."

"Well. Enough." Obermann made a visible effort to recover himself. "The anger you cause me weakens me and shortens my life. I will not indulge in it."

"I am sorry if I have distressed you."

"Are you?" He stared at Thornton. "We will be at peace then. There is an ancient Greek custom for settling an argument. The one who starts a quarrel quotes from the eighth book of the *Odyssey*. 'Farewell, respected stranger! If a harsh word has been spoken, may the winds at once catch it and carry it off!' The other replies from the eighteenth book of the *Iliad*. 'Let us let the past be over and done with, though it grieves me deeply. I will force back the anger that rises in my heart.' Can you remember the words from the *Odyssey*?"

"But I did not begin an argument, Herr Obermann. I simply stated the conclusions of my work."

"So I myself am to blame?"

"You uttered the harsh words, sir."

"So be it. It is no matter." He recited the lines from Homer and, under his prompting, Thornton replied.

"Now we are men again," Obermann said. He tried to smile at Thornton, but it seemed that he could not do so; he left him hurriedly.

Thornton himself was shaking. He sat down upon his bed, and tried to calm himself. He had taken the full force of Obermann's anger and contempt, and he knew that he could not stay at Hissarlik.

TWENTY-FIVE

Sophia found herself lying on the bed within her room in the Central Hotel at Kannakale, the wooden fan revolving slowly and noisily above her. She had considered nothing—thought of nothing—on the wild ride away from the farm. She must have slept through the night, but she had no recollection of coming back to this place.

The mad woman was Obermann's wife, whom he had married in Russia. When he had inadvertently confessed to that marriage, he had told Sophia that she had committed suicide. But she had not died. She had been kept by two of Obermann's Greek servants, travelling with him from Greece to Asia Minor. Leonid was Obermann's son. Already she began to see resemblances between them that she had not noticed before—the set of the jaw, the broad forehead.

She knew all this as clearly and as plainly as if she had been told by her husband himself. Her husband? There was no likelihood that he had divorced the mad woman, in which case Sophia had never been lawfully married to him. She turned over in the bed, and moaned. Who was she now? What was she now? She could see nothing ahead of her except darkness, and she was lost. She got up and washed her face with water from a bowl and pitcher next to her bed.

Her first thought now was to flee—to flee from him, to flee from herself, to flee from Troy. If she returned to Athens she would be disgraced, of course, but this fate did not displease her. She knew that she could not rely upon her mother's sense of honour, where finances were concerned, but she believed that she could withstand her reproaches. As for her father, well, her father did not matter. She flung herself down upon the bed once more and wept.

But then, without in the least expecting or intending anything, she stopped crying. She wiped her eyes with the sleeve of her jacket, and stood up. Her anxiety and helplessness were lifted from her, and instead she sensed her anger. He had lied to her. He had hidden from her "the history," as he had called it in the letter to Theodore Skopelos. He had violated and betrayed her. "I will not be fearful," she said out loud. "I will not be meek. I will not be destroyed. I will fight him and win." She would not flee. She would return to Hissarlik, and confront him. She would use Thornton and Lineau as witnesses in her accusations against him. Why should she become the victim of his deception, when she had a will as strong as his and a conscience infinitely more pure? She went down into the courtyard, having told the staff of the hotel that she would reserve the room for an indefinite period, and collected her horse. Then she began the journey to Hissarlik.

—◦◦◦—

THEY HAD WARNED HER, in the hotel, of the approaching storm. The sky was dark, and a fierce wind blew from the sea. There was a lightning flash as she left the town, followed by slow thunder. In her eager and alert state, the lightning seemed to take the form of an arrow, pointing her towards Troy. Her horse flared its nostrils and arched its neck apprehensively, but Sophia urged it forward. When the rain came, she laughed aloud. Within seconds her clothes were as sodden as if she had walked into the sea, but she scarcely noticed. Her spirit was still fiery.

When she came up to the Scamander, the river was hurtling along its course and ahead of her she could see the great mound of

Hissarlik veiled in the downpour, the vapour issuing from it like smoke. She spurred her horse forward once more, eager to confront Obermann with the full fury of the elements around her, and she quickly rode up to the site of the excavations. But then she stopped, surprised at what she saw. Alexander Thornton's quarters had been touched by some kind of fire, and the thatched roof had been destroyed. The intense rain was pouring into its interior. She dismounted and ran towards it. As she approached the threshold she saw that the door was swinging open and Thornton himself suddenly appeared; he was slightly bowed, as if in pain, and he did not seem to notice her. "Alexander! Alexander! What has happened?"

"Everything has gone. Washed away. Destroyed."

"The tablets?"

"Yes."

She looked up at the charred and still smouldering thatch. "It must have been the lightning," she said. "I saw it over Kannakale." Sophia glanced around for Obermann. She could see him in the distance, behind a ridge, superintending the covering of the stones with canvas cloths.

"I cannot say if lightning was responsible. I cannot say that." He gazed at her steadily, and at once she understood what he meant. He suspected some human agency. "I woke up to the heat of the flames. Just before this terrible storm broke around us. But I had no chance to save them. The rain——" He looked for a moment as if he were about to weep. "Everything gone. My drawings, too. They have been destroyed."

"Let me see."

He took her inside, and she saw the tablets reduced to glutinous dark brown clay. Thornton's drawings had been charred by flame and soaked by the tempest.

"Everything destroyed," he said again. "As if the tablets had never been." The torrent still fell upon them. "That is what he wanted."

Sophia peered into the remains of Thornton's quarters, in the hope that some tablets or drawings had survived. Then she sensed a slight movement on Thornton's bed, and turned her head towards it;

a small brown adder was moving across his pillow. She took his arm and pointed. "Look. There. The snake. *Antelion*." It writhed over the white linen cloth, and they both stepped back. "We must leave this place," she said urgently. "We must leave now."

"But your husband—"

"He is not my husband!" she whispered to him then, as if she could hardly trust her own words. "He is trying to kill you."

"What?"

"The snake. It will not have been here by chance. I know that he seeks them out."

For the first time he appeared to be frightened. "What shall we do?"

"Come. We must go now. He has not seen us."

"But my—"

"Take your passport and all your money. I will join you in moments."

She ran to the quarters that she shared with Obermann. He was still busily occupied with the preservation of the site from the storm, and had not noticed her arrival. She rushed into the little hut, and retrieved the jewels that she had brought with her from Athens before running out again into the storm.

Thornton was waiting for her, alerted by her energy and determination to leave Troy. "Take a horse," she shouted, "and follow me."

Then they rode in the streaming rain towards Kannakale. Another lightning flash lit up the plain. It had become a marsh, with a ridge of hard ground on which they rode. The rain veiled their retreat so that no one saw them leave, except the boy who ran errands for Obermann.

———

WHEN THEY ARRIVED at the Central Hotel, the proprietor looked at them with alarm. He spoke to Sophia in Greek. "Madame Obermann, why do you ride through this fearful storm?"

"There has been a fire," she said. "We are here for refuge."

"A fire? Was there injury?"

"No, none whatever. Do you have a room for Mr. Thornton? He is an Englishman, working for Heinrich Obermann." She pronounced the name very crisply.

"Of course. Now you must dry yourself and change your clothes. The storms of this region cause sickness."

They were given towels as soon as they entered their rooms. Thornton was lent the blouse and wide trousers of the Turkish workman, and Sophia dressed herself in the black garb of the local women.

"We are natives," she said, as soon as Thornton had opened the door of his room to her. "Does it suit me?"

He was surprised by her gaiety in these circumstances. "You have no fever, I hope."

"Fever? I have never felt so well in my life!" She laughed at his expression of concern. "We have made a decision."

He pulled up a chair for her, and sat opposite to her. "Do you know what we have done?"

"Of course. We have slain the dragon."

"We can never go back."

"Do you really wish to go back? He tried to kill you."

"The snake may have entered during the storm."

"He has destroyed the tablets."

"That may have been an accident, Sophia."

"There are no accidents in Troy." They were speaking rapidly and urgently to one another.

"You said that he was not your husband."

Then she told him the story, to which he listened with great attention.

When she had finished, he sighed. "So he has brought this woman—"

"His wife."

"He has brought his wife with him in the care of servants. I wonder how she lost her mind."

"I do not wish to know."

"And are you sure that Leonid is her son?"

"He called her Mother, Alexander. I think that is proof enough, don't you?"

"He does resemble Obermann. I see that now. But I never guessed—"

"No one could have guessed it."

"Of course, that is why he calls him Telemachus. The son of wily Odysseus."

"I wanted to confront him. To attack him. But you are right. I cannot go back."

At that moment the strangeness of Thornton's situation became obvious to him. "I have no reason to go back. He has destroyed my work. If we had been seen to leave—"

"It would be compromising?"

"Naturally."

"For a man and a woman to ride off in a storm?"

"And," he said, "he will soon know that our passports and money have gone with us."

She stood up, and went over to the window. The torrent still fell upon the deserted streets of Kannakale. "We will go to Constantinople. There we will be invisible until we decide what to do. You must return to England, of course."

"And you, Sophia?"

"I have no notion."

"Will you go back to Greece?"

"I have been Obermann's whore." Thornton blushed deeply. "Who will want me there? My parents have relied upon his money. They will not thank me for returning."

"We can be married, Sophia." He said it lightly, almost casually. "I might say that it is to save your reputation, but that would be an insult to you. I wish to marry you." She turned back from the window, and stared at him. "I know a clergyman in London who will be sympathetic. No one knows you there."

"No one knows my *history*? But I will be a hindrance to you."

"I cannot think of a more agreeable fate."

She believed that he was offering to marry her out of sympathy, to give her legal status and a name. "Is it easy to be granted a divorce in England, after a decent interval?"

"I have said nothing about divorcing you."

She looked at him, uncertain how to respond. "I don't understand you, Alexander."

"I am happy for you to be my wife. I want you to be my wife."

"But we scarcely know one another."

"I have watched you, Sophia, as I once told you. I have seen you in the shadow of that man. I have talked to you. I have shared my discoveries with you, and seen the same enthusiasm in your eyes. That place is like some testing ground. I know you as well now as if I had known you for a hundred years."

"A hundred years would be too long." She did not know how to respond to him. "We would have tired of each other."

"I could never tire of you."

"I am not a virgin, Alexander."

"Are you carrying his child?"

"No. I think not."

"That is enough for me."

"And what of him?" she asked.

"He will bark and bluster," Thornton replied, "but he will do nothing. It would be intolerable to his pride to let it be known."

"He is a bigamist. In Greek law he would be imprisoned." She hesitated for a moment. "But what if he had divorced the Russian woman?"

"He cannot have divorced her for the reason of insanity. There is no such plea. That is the case in England." He was thinking of one of his colleagues in the museum, who had been obliged to place his wife in a private mad-house in Hoxton. "Would he keep her close, in the care of his own servants, if he had long since divorced her? It is over, Sophia. You will never see him again." During the course of this conversation they had steadily drawn closer. They might have touched, but they did not.

"And your work?" she asked him.

"My work here is over. I am sure that I can repeat from memory many of the symbols, but what kind of evidence is that? They might have come from an over-eager imagination. I have no proof or record of any kind."

"But surely you can explain what you believe?"

"It would be a foolish exercise, Sophia. Obermann would laugh at me."

"Do you think that he deliberately destroyed everything?"

"Otherwise, as you say, there is too much coincidence. I heard the thatch catch fire moments before the storm broke. I was aware of no lightning flash. I saw nothing of the kind. What could have been easier for him than to set fire to the thatch when he saw the rains coming?"

"In that atmosphere a lighted candle would have been enough."

He leaned over and, for the first time, kissed her lightly on the forehead. "And you believe that he introduced the snake?"

"He watches those snakes with glee. He loves their deadliness."

"There were enough cracks and fissures in the stone for one to crawl through. But why kill me?"

"Don't you see? He is a child. He cannot bear contradiction. He cannot bear rivals."

"He could not endure the thought of Troy—"

"His Troy, Alexander."

"Of his Troy being demolished. He saw an army of Homeric heroes. I saw a tribe of alien people who cultivated human sacrifice."

"That was intolerable for him. Troy has become his very existence."

"What will he do now?"

"He will carry on working. He will not rest. When he has revealed the whole of the ancient city, he will move on. He will find some other sacred place."

"He will dismiss the tablets as if they had never existed."

"He will have forgotten them already." She shivered suddenly. "The rain has penetrated us."

TWENTY-SIX

Obermann had been busy preserving the excavations from the fury of the storm, and the entire day had been occupied in laying down sheets of canvas as well as makeshift shelters of wood and corrugated metal. "Now," he said to Lineau, "it looks like the battleground of Sebastopol. But we have defeated the enemy." He was looking at Thornton's burned and damaged hut. "I have not seen Mr. Thornton since the tragedy. He will be desolate."

"So are we all. Kadri Bey tells me that the lightning has destroyed everything."

"Where the rain entered there is only mud. You have been to Thornton's quarters?"

"I could not bring myself to enter. I could not bear the waste of all his hopes."

"Your sensitivity does you credit, Lineau. Yet I wonder why he has not appeared. I will send the boy to him."

"The English are prone to self-slaughter."

"I doubt if that is Thornton's case. He is too stubborn. Rashid, come here. Call Mr. Thornton. He is unhappy. If he is not there, see if he is wandering among the rocks. But be careful. The storms bring out the snakes."

Rashid shook his head. "He is gone, sir."

"Gone? Gone where?"

"He was on horseback. Madame was travelling with him. Towards Kannakale."

"You must be dreaming, Rashid. Madame is already in the town. She left yesterday." Again the boy shook his head. "Very well. I will investigate the mysterious disappearance of Alexander Thornton."

He walked over to Thornton's quarters, now ruined and partly open to the sky, and as soon as he entered he knew that the Englishman had gone. Although he had laughed at Lineau's mention of the English tendency to suicide, he looked carefully in the little alcove off the main room. "He has fled," he said to himself. "Well done." And then he thought of Sophia. It was impossible that she should have returned and left again, so swiftly and so silently.

He heard the sound of Leonid's horse before he saw Leonid himself, exhausted and sodden with rain. "You should have stayed at the farm, Telemachus. There was no need to ride through the storm."

"Every need."

———

LEONID HAD DELAYED his departure from the farm of Theodore Skopelos. He feared his father's wrath. As soon as Sophia had seen him with his mother, he knew that everything would change. He had not meant to disclose that the woman was his mother, but he had called to Sophia by instinct. He could not deny the connection. He loved his mother, even in her madness, and could not betray her in her presence. So he had stayed that night at the farm, considering the best course of action. Even though the storm had begun on the following morning, he knew that he had to return to Troy and face the consequences of his disclosure.

———

"WHAT IS THE MATTER with you, Telemachus? You look as if you are about to be hanged."

"I have something to tell you."

"Well, what is it?"

"Sophia has visited the farm."

"I know it. She travelled there two months ago. What of it?"

"She came again yesterday. Unexpectedly."

"Oh?"

"She saw Elena."

"I beg your pardon?"

"She knows." Obermann stared wildly around at the excavations. "She came upon us quietly. She heard me call her Mother."

Obermann walked a short distance away, and bowed his head as if he were in profound thought. Then he raised his face to the sky and let out a great cry of horror and anguish that startled the Turkish workers. It was rumoured among them that Herr Obermann had lost many treasures during the rainstorm. When he came back to Leonid, he was more composed. "When precisely did this happen?"

"In the late afternoon."

"Yet you have waited this long to return."

"I was ashamed."

Obermann hit him hard on the side of his face. "Never feel shame, Telemachus. Feel grief. Feel sorrow. But never feel shame. It is the enemy."

Even as he spoke he began to understand what had happened. Rashid had been right. Sophia had returned to Troy, in her anger, and had encountered Thornton. They had decided to flee together—to flee Obermann, and to flee Troy. Their rage and their despair had united them against him. It was as clear as if he had heard every word spoken between them.

"How was your mother?"

"She was excited by the sight of Sophia. She could not sleep."

"Yes. Sophia has that effect on others." He called for Rashid, and asked him to repeat what the boy had already told him. "They were on two horses, you say?" The boy nodded. "And they were riding to-wards Kannakale. You are sure of that?"

"They took the old path. I watched them until the rain hid them."

"You must go to Kannakale, Rashid, and find them. Do not

approach them. Say nothing to them. But discover where they are hiding and then return to me. Do you understand?"

"Yes, sir. May I take Pegasus? He is swift."

"Ride like the wind, Rashid. I expect you to return before night-fall." The boy ran off, delighted by the chance to ride the Barbary. "Well, Telemachus, what is your plan?"

"It is not for me—"

"No, Telemachus. It is not for you to say. You have done enough harm."

"That is unfair, sir. You insist that I visit her. You will not see her yourself. Am I to blame that she is my mother?"

"Softly, softly. There is no blame. I know that. This is the pattern of the Fates. They alone dare oppose the sovereign will of Zeus. Clotho spins the thread. Lachesis weaves it. And Atropos cuts it."

Leonid looked at him barely able to conceal his surprise. "And you are Zeus?"

"We are all gods, Telemachus, when the occasion demands it." He said nothing for a moment, digging the tip of his shoe into the loose earth. "Did your mother realise that Sophia—"

"Who knows what the mad understand? She howled after she had gone."

Obermann put his hand up to his face. "She is not spared grief, even as she is."

———

AT DINNER THAT NIGHT, with Lineau and Kadri Bey, Ober-mann seemed to Leonid to be particularly animated. He remarked upon the absence of Alexander Thornton, explaining to them that he had spoken with the Englishman shortly before his departure. He had decided to return to England. Mr. Thornton had travelled to Kan-nakale in order to arrange transport at the shipping office for his jour-ney. Sophia had been detained, no doubt waiting for news after the storm, but she would arrive soon. On this matter Lineau and Kadri Bey were silent. Both men suspected another explanation for the Englishman's absence with Frau Obermann. But, of course, they could not speak of it. "He has no wish to remain here," Obermann was saying. "The loss of the tablets has affected him deeply."

"It has affected us all," Kadri Bey replied. "It is the greatest blow we have suffered here."

"There are elements of tragedy in this." Lineau seemed to be staring straight ahead. "It is difficult to comprehend what it means."

"Why so melancholy, gentlemen? For all we know, they were only the lists of goods."

"Only?" Lineau turned towards Obermann, who was momentarily unsettled by his sightless gaze. "It was our first glimpse into an unknown world. It was a momentous discovery."

"And who is to say that we will not find more?"

"If any have survived the storm."

"There will be other sites and other places where they lie concealed. Be more cheerful, Lineau. All is not lost. All my life I have retained my optimism. That is why I have been so successful."

"Can nothing of them be recovered?" Kadri Bey asked him. "Have Mr. Thornton's notes been saved?"

"Alas not. His notes were scattered in the storm. Those we have found are illegible. Have some more of these anchovies, Lineau. Telemachus, you have hardly eaten."

"I am not hungry, sir."

"The tragedy has taken away your appetite. It will return by the morning." At this moment Rashid came running up to them. He was about to approach Obermann, but he waved the boy away. "Shall I propose a toast?"

"We have something to celebrate?" Kadri Bey looked at him in surprise.

"A toast to Alexander Thornton! May he live to gain world renown!" Leonid looked at him oddly, but he raised his glass. "It is wonderful, gentlemen, that in the midst of this terrible disaster and sorrow we can be gay! The atmosphere of Troy revives us."

"It has seen greater sorrows," Lineau said.

"Precisely. Here we are part of the world soul. Excuse me for a moment." He walked over to Rashid, who was standing by Thornton's quarters. "Well. What have you discovered?"

"They are staying in the Central."

"Have you spoken to Hasad?" Hasad Dumanek was the proprietor of the Central Hotel, whom Obermann had favoured with many small gifts from the excavations.

"Madame is in room ten. The Englishman is in room four."

"What else?"

"She has paid for one week in English sterling."

"That will be from Mr. Thornton's purse."

"She has been asking for details of the boats to Constantinople."

"Constantinople? Is that their destination? They are fools. Do they think that I cannot reach them? They left in a storm. They will be enveloped in a storm." He came closer to Rashid. "Say nothing to anyone. If you mention one word, I shall cut out your tongue."

The boy ran off, impressed by this warning, and Obermann returned to the others. "Rashid tells me that the market at Kannakale has been flooded. We must exist without fruit for a day or two. It is fortunate that there are fewer mouths to feed this evening."

—◦◦◦—

AFTER THE MEAL was over, and the others had retired, Obermann remained talking to Leonid. "I am inclined to think," Obermann said, "that the stones we found by the stream are part of a temple. When the stream was in torrent this morning, it took a natural curve away from the site. There is solid masonry blocking the watercourse." Leonid was surprised that, in the general confusion of the storm, Obermann had noticed this. The site had been surveyed only two days before. "The men must begin work there in the morning, Telemachus. We must lose no time. There will be an altar."

Leonid could no longer restrain his impatience. "What did Rashid tell you?"

"They have separate rooms in the hotel, and have paid for a week in advance. They are planning to travel to Constantinople."

"Where they can disappear."

"It will not be so easy for them. I have many friends in the city. They will be seen. I believe that they will try to sail for England."

"Try?"

Obermann waved the question aside. "It has just occurred to me that they may seek a legal wedding at sea." He got up suddenly, and paced around the table. "Now that she has seen your mother—" He stopped for a moment, and poured himself another glass of wine. "Women know. Women have the instinct."

"No captain would allow a marriage. They have no witnesses."

"Money is the best witness of all." He picked up his glass. "The English will not accept her. I know them. They are narrow. They do not like foreigners."

"Yet she could hide in London. It is vast and dark."

"And what kind of existence would that be for her? It would be insupportable. To live among the teeming millions? I tell you, Telemachus, she is doomed to misery if she stays with Thornton."

"Then you must rescue her."

"Of course! What a transformation that would be! To pluck her out of London and to carry her back to the sunshine of her native land." He seemed to be seriously considering the possibility. "She will tire of him very quickly. He has no spirit. No energy. He is as white as the lily." Obermann sat down heavily. "He will have very little blood."

"Do not gash him then."

Obermann laughed. "I promise you that I will set no hand upon him."

———～∿～———

THAT NIGHT, Obermann left his bed. He was still dressed, having lain awake in the hours after he had returned from dinner, and he found his shoes in the darkness. He opened the door of the hut quietly and walked into the night. The sky, now that the storm had passed, was awash with stars; the air was clear and cool, shedding a strange translucence over the stones and earth of Troy. On some of the vases he had taken from the excavations, he had seen what appeared to be the images of sun, moon and stars signified by a wheel, a circle and a cluster of dots. Priam and Hecuba had seen this sky. He walked down to the remnant of the old walls; the storm had dislodged most of the surrounding earth and debris, so that they stood solid and gleaming in the air. On such a night as this, he could sense the ancient life of Troy. On such a night, he walked through its populated streets.

He went down to the patch of partly excavated ground, where he believed that a temple had been erected near the stream. It was a tributary of the Scamander, making its way across the flat terrain immediately beneath the rising ground of Hissarlik, but after the storm it was running quickly. He could hear the sound of its waters in the night, and found the spot where the sound seemed to surround him. Here the temple, and the altar, had been erected. He raised his arms into the air and put up his face to the constellations. Then he began to chant. "Be Zeus my witness, greatest and most glorious of the gods, and you Fates who beneath the earth wreak vengeance on false men, I call upon all the gods to avenge the wrongs committed against their laws. I name Alexander Thornton and Sophia Chrysanthis. May the gods give them many woes. If any have broken the divine laws, may they be punished." It was the ritual formula he had memorised, and he knew that Homer had borrowed it from more ancient sources.

Then he fell upon his knees. "I have no sacrifice," he said, in a conversational voice, "but I pledge myself to your service." An owl hooted, from a clump of oaks beside the slope. "Pallas Athene, great goddess, daughter of Zeus who bears the aegis, you hear my prayer. Flashing-eyed Athene, whose winged words counsel the other gods, stay by my side." Then he heard the music of pipes, coming perhaps from the guards who protected the site. He rose from his knees and, in more cheerful mood, returned to the ruins of Troy.

TWENTY-SEVEN

Sophia and Alexander had booked their passage to Constantinople at the shipping office by the quay. They had elected to remain on the outside deck for the journey, in order to preserve their funds, and were returning to the hotel to collect their few possessions. Sophia needed to retrieve the case of jewels that she had placed in the hotel safe. The boat sailed in two hours. It was the first vessel heading for Constantinople, and they had purchased their tickets with some urgency. It was not clear to them what Obermann knew or guessed. But they wanted to leave this place as soon as possible. Neither of them realised that Rashid had watched them leave together.

As they crossed the square, by the entrance of the hotel, they saw him. Obermann was standing with the proprietor, Hasad Dumanek, gesticulating towards the sea.

Sophia stopped, and instinctively was about to turn back. "He must not see us," she whispered. "We can go into the market."

"No. I refuse to hide." He noticed her hesitation. "Are you afraid of him, Sophia?"

"Afraid? No. Of course not."

"We are guilty of nothing."

"You are right, of course. I see him now for what he is."

"What can he do to us? We leave in two hours. Come. We will walk across the square. Remember. We have done nothing wrong."

"He is the one who has wronged us. He should flee from *us*."

Obermann saw them, just as they left the square and advanced towards the entrance of the hotel. "My two friends!" He called to them, and extended his arms. "I have been looking for you. I have been concerned for you. By great good fortune I have met Hasad, who tells me you are safe and well."

"We are well, Heinrich."

"The gods are protecting you, Sophia. But I have missed you dreadfully. It is time to come back, is it not?"

She shook her head. "No. I will not come back."

"Is 'not' a word to use to your husband?"

"You are not my husband. And you are aware of that."

Obermann was struck with apparent wonder. "Have the laws of the world been overturned? Have I been sleeping?"

"Has not Leonid told you that I have seen your wife? I have seen Frau Obermann."

"Telemachus is so forgetful. He tells me nothing."

"That is strange. Since he is your son."

Obermann looked at her, and laughed. "You are like the oracle, Sophia. You speak more than you understand."

"I understand that you have lied to me and deceived me and betrayed me."

"Not so loud."

"I will shout it from the highest building." She was becoming steadily more angry as she spoke.

"Not in this place, Sophia."

"This is the perfect place. The public square is used to accuse adulterers, is it not?"

"Harsh words. Not deserved. You are my wife in the eyes of the gods. They have blessed our union. The human law is of no consequence."

"Your gods do not exist, Heinrich."

"Be sure that you are not struck down."

"They are a figment of your imagination. Of your pride."

"I suppose that you have taught her this, Mr. Thornton?" Obermann turned upon Thornton. "You have steadily undermined me and ridiculed my beliefs."

"I need no lessons, Heinrich."

"I have never mocked you, Herr Obermann. I had the greatest respect for you."

"But you respect my wife more, I see."

"I am not your wife."

Two or three inhabitants of the town had stopped to watch this argument among the foreigners. Hasad glanced anxiously at them, and guided Sophia and Thornton across the road back into the square. "We must have no problem," he said. "No problem near the hotel. The other guests—"

Obermann walked after them, shaking his head, as if he pitied them. "I have done nothing against my conscience," he said. "I have done no wrong."

"You lied to me."

"The woman you saw is dead to me. She is as good as dead. Telemachus did not wish her to be placed in an asylum. That is all."

"We sail in two hours," Sophia said.

"If you leave me now, you leave me for ever. You understand that."

"Of course."

"We must prepare," Thornton said. "Time is pressing."

"And who will believe your own lies, Mr. Thornton? You will return to London and tell them that Troy was the home of Asiatics and cannibals. There is no one who could possibly accept such a theory. It is preposterous. It is without proof."

"You destroyed that proof."

"I am the fire. I am the storm. I am the rain. Is that the sum of your conclusions? They will laugh at you."

"I have no intention of discussing the tablets with anyone."

"Ah, a miracle of silence!"

"But I am sure that evidence will appear elsewhere."

"You will keep your powder dry. Is that it, Mr. Thornton?"

"I will draw up a memoir that will only be published if incontrovertible proof of my speculations emerges from another quarter."

"Bravo! Nobly put!" He turned back to Sophia. "Where are you sailing?" She looked briefly at Thornton. "There is no need to hesitate, Sophia. I will know the details of your journey within seconds of your leaving."

"We are travelling to Constantinople."

"The city of the flowers. The city of gold. As a young man, Mr. Thornton, I loved gold. When I was a merchant in St. Petersburg, I delighted in the worn coin passing from hand to hand. Did you know that I was once a banker buying gold dust in California? One evening, after drinking my German beer, I covered my face with the precious dust so that it became a golden mask!"

"And thus you became a great king," Sophia said.

"I knew that already. I knew that I had something within me that would lift me upwards. How will you live in Constantinople?"

"We will live," she said.

"And from there you will journey to London. Am I right?"

"That is my home, sir."

"The British Museum will be overjoyed, Mr. Thornton, to see your safe return. You have survived the legendary monster Obermann. You will be a hero!"

"I doubt I will be called that."

"But you will bring back with you a prize beyond price." Obermann was about to put his hand on Sophia's shoulder, but she turned away.

"I am not a prize, Heinrich. Alexander has not won me. I go with him from my own will and wish."

"Bravo! But you delude yourself, Sophia. You will not find any happiness in England. When you were working in Troy, you were content. I remember the look of joy when you uncovered the staircase."

"Don't you understand? I was doing it for you."

"For me?" He seemed puzzled for a moment.

"Yes, Heinrich. For you."

"Are you telling me that you loved me, Sophia?"

"I cannot answer that."

"We must go back to the hotel," Thornton said to her. "We must get to the ship very soon." He took her arm and, without saying anything more to Obermann, they crossed the street in front of the square.

Obermann watched them, then suddenly ran towards them. "Did you love me, Sophia?"

TWENTY-EIGHT

Leonid had decided to ride at once to Kannakale. Early that morning, just after Obermann had left for the town, a discovery had been made. The heavy rains had dislodged a great pile of stones and rubble during the storm, disclosing the entrance to a stone-built chamber at the south-west of the palace complex; two workmen had entered it, clearing away some of the detritus that remained, and had then run out to announce their discovery. They had seen hundreds, and perhaps thousands, of clay tablets stacked neatly against the interior walls. Leonid had joined them and, on entering the dark enclosed space, could make out the piles of tablets; he lit a Lucifer match and, in the flickering light, he could see the same signs and markings that Thornton had been attempting to decipher. The Englishman's work could be revived after the disaster of the storm.

Kadri Bey had at once given orders for the objects to be removed and preserved in a place of safety. Leonid, sensing the significance of the find to Thornton and to Obermann, knew that he should go to Kannakale. The tablets themselves might offer a way of resolving their argument. If Thornton returned to Troy, his sudden flight with Sophia might be conveniently forgotten or explained. Leonid might even reach the Englishman before any confrontation with his father.

So he took Pegasus and galloped over the plain, his excitement and sense of urgency increasing as he came closer to the town.

When he arrived at Kannakale, he rode fast down the thoroughfare from the eastern gate, and turned the corner that led to the public square; he saw the hotel to his right, but he did not rein in his horse. Then suddenly someone ran in front of him. Pegasus reared up in alarm, and struck the running man with its forelegs. He went down at once, under the frightened animal; it reared up again, and its hooves came down heavily upon the prostrate body. In that moment of consternation Leonid heard a woman scream.

——∿∿——

SOPHIA HAD TURNED, at the sound of the horse's alarm, to see Obermann being struck and hurled to the ground. She watched in horror as Pegasus trampled upon his body. Leonid jumped down, and ran back to find the injured and bloodied body of his father lying in the mud of the public thoroughfare. The shock of discovery and recognition seemed to drive him backward; he staggered against a wooden post by the side of the road, and looked blankly at Sophia and Thornton as they ran over to the fallen man. Then he watched as two townsmen caught hold of the reins of the horse and led it into the square.

"We must carry him to the hotel," Sophia was saying. "Call a doctor to him at once." Obermann was not moving. One of his arms was stretched out at an unnatural angle, and his head was broken where the hooves of the horse had caught him. His forehead was an open wound. Blood covered his face, and continued to run into the mud. "Take him up," Sophia urged Thornton and Hasad, who were standing beside her in confusion. "Take him up and call for help."

Hasad took his shoulders and Thornton his legs; they might have been carrying a bundle of clothes, so little life was there, and Obermann's arm dangled down like some broken wing. With difficulty they carried him into the hotel, and placed him on a divan in the vestibule. Hasad indicated, with alarm, that the green silk was soon soaked with Obermann's blood. "He cannot live," he said.

Sophia had gone over to Leonid and had put her arm around his shoulders. "You could do nothing," she murmured to him. "I saw. He ran into your path."

"He is my father."

"I know that. But it was not your fault. He did not see you. Come now, Leonid. We must help him."

They hurried into the hotel. "I have called for a doctor," Hasad told them, as soon as they entered. "But—" He looked at Leonid.

"He is dead?" Leonid asked him.

"I cannot be sure. But I can see no movement."

Thornton was bent over the body. He took up Obermann's hand and wrist. "There is no pulse," he said. "I do not think any doctor can save him now."

"We must wait," Hasad said. "He is a Greek doctor. Very skilled."

"Is there nothing we can do for him?" Sophia went over to the divan. The blood had begun to congeal, and she could glimpse the face of the dead man. She could tell that Obermann had gone for ever, and she was surprised by her own tears. She had been running away from him, but this unexpected parting caused her the keenest distress. Was this the meaning of tragedy? When a life is filled with light for a moment, and then the moment passes into darkness?

———

THE DOCTOR gave only the most cursory inspection of the body. "There is no life here," he said. "It is useless to minister to him now. My apologies." He walked over to Hasad, who was standing by the doorway of the hotel. "My only task is to complete the death certificate. I can do no more."

"There will be a hearing?"

"No need. These people are witnesses to the accident?" Hasad nodded. "The circumstances are clear enough." The doctor turned back to look at Sophia, who was still standing beside the body. "So that was the great Obermann. He disappeared in an instant."

Leonid had been sitting on a small gilt chair in the vestibule, his hands up to his face. He had been weeping, but now he stood up and walked over to Sophia. "He must be taken back to Troy," he told her. "That is what he wished."

"How do you know that?"

"He talked of it once. He talked of his funeral pyre in the city. He wished his ashes to be scattered over the Scamander." He looked at the body of his father. "I cannot bear to see him like this. We must cover him. We must carry him home." He walked over to Hasad, and spoke to him quietly for a few moments. "It is done," he said. "Hasad will lend us the coach he reserves for his favoured guests."

A few minutes later an old-fashioned landau, painted in scarlet and yellow, drew up in front of the hotel; it was pulled by two horses, bedecked in the same colours. But before the body of Obermann could be moved from the divan by Leonid and Thornton, Hasad prevented them. "Wait one moment," he said to them. He called to his wife, who was standing in the rear office of the hotel, and briefly spoke to her. Within a few minutes she had come back with a female servant. They were carrying armfuls of fresh rushes, which they scattered upon the floor of the landau. Then Leonid and Thornton carried the body into the street. A crowd of townspeople had gathered outside and, when Obermann emerged, the women began wailing a funereal lament. The two men placed him carefully on the rushes, and Hasad's wife then came forward to place more rushes upon the body itself so that it was covered with a blanket of green.

"Are you coming with me?" Leonid asked Sophia and Thornton.

Sophia was the one who replied. "Of course," she said. "We will return to Troy."

——⁓——

ON THEIR ARRIVAL at the excavations, they were met by Lineau and Kadri Bey. The two men had seen the brightly coloured landau crossing the plain, and had known at once that something had happened. They were silent, as Leonid dismounted and helped Sophia out of the carriage. They had glimpsed the body of Obermann beneath the rushes. Kadri Bey murmured a prayer, and put his head into his hands. Lineau turned away.

"There has been an accident," Sophia said. "Horrible. Terrible."

Thornton stepped down from the vehicle and walked over to Lineau. He put his arm around the Frenchman, who muttered some words of Greek.

"What was that?"

"From the twentieth book of the *Iliad*. Heinrich often used to quote it. 'Achilles will suffer whatever Fate has spun for him, at the time of his birth when his mother bore him.' "

"It was not Fate. It was chance, Lineau."

"Heinrich would not have thought so. For him it was resistless Fate. You know that Leonid was his son?"

"Yes. Sophia discovered the truth of it. How long have you known?"

"Many years. We never spoke of it, of course. I should have warned Sophia, perhaps. But by the time she arrived here, she had become his wife. It was too late."

"Not his wife. No. He was already married."

"He had not divorced Elena?"

"We do not think so."

"So he wove his own destructive fate. Poor man." Lineau sighed. "You know that we have found more tablets?"

"I beg your pardon?"

"We have found hundreds of the baked-clay tablets, just like those you examined. You have work to do, my friend. You and Sophia."

———◇———

SOPHIA WAS STANDING with Leonid as the body was taken from the landau by the Turkish workers.

"It is over," Leonid said. "Troy without Obermann is not Troy."

"There is still work to be done."

"But he knew the heart of Troy. Its life. He held us in its enchantment."

"That enchantment will return."

"No. Never more."

"What will you do?"

"I will go back to Russia. With my mother. I will care for her there. I could not bear to live in this place now. In the presence of my father every stone seemed blessed. Every tree harboured a god."

"So you believed his stories?"

"Of course. They had the truth of vision. What is the world without vision? Well, I will find out now."

"And so will I."

IN THE HEAT and humidity, there could be no delay. And so the ceremony was conducted that same evening before sunset. There was no need for a minister since, as Leonid said, Obermann had not believed in the religion of priests.

The men and women who had worked at the excavations lined up in two processional rows, between which Obermann was carried to a great mound placed in the centre of the palace courtyard. The pyre was constructed of wood and cloths soaked with naphtha, upon which Leonid, Thornton and Kadri Bey placed the body. Thornton then read out the words of the Twenty-seventh Psalm, from the Bible that he had brought with him from England, and Kadri Bey recited part of the fifth chapter of the Koran. Leonid then lit the pyre with a flaming brand. The cloths and the wood burned quickly, and Obermann was enveloped in flame. The constant wind had dropped. The watchers remained silent as a thin column of smoke rose towards the cloudless sky. The ripple of the burning air, above the flames, seemed to Sophia to take the shape of dancers.

"I will miss you," she whispered. "Memory eternal, Heinrich."

From the range of Mount Ida, there came a sudden peal of thunder.

ALSO BY PETER ACKROYD

*"Magnificent. . . . Succeeds in
animating on the page the life of one of the oldest
and greatest . . . cities in the world."*
—The New York Times Book Review

LONDON
The Biography

Here are two thousand years of London's history and
folklore, its chroniclers and criminals and plain citizens,
its food and drink and countless pleasures. Blackfriars
and Charing Cross, Paddington and Bedlam. Westminster
Abbey and St. Martin-in-the-Fields. Cockney and va-
grants. Immigrants, peasants, and punks. The Plague, the
Great Fire, and the Blitz. London at all times of day and
night, and in all kinds of weather. Through a unique the-
matic tour of the physical city and its inimitable soul, the
city comes alive.

History/978-0-385-49771-8

ALSO AVAILABLE
Albion, 978-0-385-49773-2
The Clerkenwell Tales, 978-1-4000-7595-9
The Lambs of London, 978-1-4000-7958-2
The Life of Thomas More, 978-0-385-49693-3
The Plato Papers, 978-0-385-49769-5
Shakespeare, 978-1-4000-7598-0